BR KEN
WORLDS

ANITHA ROBINSON

Children's Brains are Yummy Books
Dallas, TX

Broken Worlds

Exploded World: Mircea Maties/Shutterstock.com
Girl: absolute-india/Shutterstock.com
Glass: ConstantinosZ/Shutterstock.com

Children's Brains are Yummy Books
Dallas, Texas
www.cbaybooks.com

Printed in the United States of America.

ISBN: 978-1-933767-37-6
ISBN: 978-1-933767-38-3 (ebook)

To my wonderful family, who inspire me everyday by following their dreams and believing in mine.

ONE

We're almost at the end of the poorly lit alley when I realize it leads nowhere. I should have kept to the main roads, even though it takes longer. Sammy hasn't said a coherent word in the last several minutes. He's so cold. His lips are chapped and colorless. I bend down and cocoon him within my arm, sharing whatever body heat I have left. He practically disappears, reminding me how small he truly is.

I have made a terrible mistake. What was I thinking? This isn't a shortcut. I turn around to head back out and see the orange glint of a cigarette. A stranger leans against one of the windowless buildings. Even in the faint light, I can see the whites of his eyes as he leers at us. He steps toward us and tosses the cigarette to the ground. A malicious smile forms on his face.

"Ow," Sammy whines, trying to wriggle his fingers free from my tightening grip.

Rooted to the spot, I look around, desperate for an escape route. My chest tightens. It's hard to breathe. The only way out is past the stranger.

I quicken my pace, pulling Sammy in close. His short legs scuttle beside me. I square my shoulders, hoping I appear unaffected by the man's sudden appearance.

1

"Please let us pass. Oh, please let us pass," I mutter under my breath.

"Did you say something?" the stranger asks.

Eyes staring straight ahead, I force myself to walk toward him. I can hear Sammy whimpering my name. "Kalli, Kalli, Kalli."

"Did you say something to me?" the stranger says again.

"No," I squeak back, annoyed that my voice sounds so small. The distance between us shrinks. He reeks of cigarette smoke.

"Kalli," gasps Sammy.

"It's okay," I whisper.

In the fading light, I can see that the guy's about my height but much heavier. His neck is huge, as wide as his head. "Where you goin' in such a hurry?" He straightens and steps out in front of me.

"Meeting our friends." I hope it sounds braver than I feel. "They're just over there." I point to a spot behind him.

"Yeah? I don't see no one there." He doesn't even look. Instead, he moves so close to me that I can see the deep acne pits that scar his cheeks.

"Bradley!" I automatically scream a name that was once so familiar.

The stranger grabs me, spins me around, and shoves me face first against the wall. Sammy's grip tightens, and I unintentionally pull him with me. He groans as his tiny body collides with the bricks.

"Please let us go. Our friends will be back any minute. I promise I won't say anything to them." I will away the

2

tears. I have to be strong for Sammy.

The man twists my arm behind my back and smacks me even harder into the wall. My flimsy winter coat is a poor barrier and the rough bricks scrape against my chest. Tears blur my vision, but I can't brush them away. I feel a cold sharp edge pressing under my chin and I'm instantly frozen with fear. A knife!

He leans into the wall so that his scarred face is level with mine. "You won't be sayin' nothin' to anyone."

I try to scream again, but there is no sound, just a dry rush of air.

Sammy starts to cry. It begins as a low whimper, but quickly escalates.

"Shut up you!" He lowers the knife from my chin. "Looks like the little shit will have to go first."

The pressure against my back lessens as he leans toward Sammy. I have to protect him. I wriggle my hand free from Sammy's grip. Before his tiny fingers can grab back, I pull and push and twist myself until my back is now against the wall. I thrash my legs and my knee finds its mark between his legs.

He slouches over, and I pull myself free. I drag Sammy along as I sprint toward the safety of the street.

"Kalli?" whimpers Sammy.

"It's going to be okay, Sammy," I pant, knowing without even looking at him that his brown eyes are huge. "Just keep running, and don't let go of my hand."

We're about fifty feet from the exit. The alleyway is getting brighter.

"Almost there—"

My right ankle is yanked backward. I crash to the concrete, pulling Sammy down with me.

"Think you could get away that easily? You stupid bitch!"

"Kalli," Sammy moans beside me.

"Sammy, run, just run!" I push him up.

"Like hell he's going to run," croaks the stranger. He drags Sammy back.

The stranger still has my right ankle, so I kick with my left foot and thrash until I hear him groan. I see Sammy crawling away.

"Sammy! Go! Run!"

"No, Kalli, not without you. You told me to not let go of your hand." He reaches back for me.

"Just go!" I scream at him. "Get help. Please, Sammy."

Even though his cheeks are covered with tears, his expression hardens. His eyes narrow and his eyebrows furrow into a straight line. He knows what must come next. I will fight, and he will flee. It's our only chance to make it.

He barely takes two steps when he trips and screams. Why can't anyone else hear him? The creep still has my right ankle, so I push up as hard as I can with my arms, and fling myself around. My ankle snaps. Ignoring the pain, I smash my left foot into the side of his head as Sammy struggles to get up.

"Come back, you little shit," my attacker snarls.

I keep punching, desperate to give Sammy a chance to run away, to escape. Sammy gives me one last look. My eyes plead with him to go. And finally, he does.

A guttural sound comes from the assailant. He drags me back deeper into the alley. I steal one final glance of Sammy running away from us, his black curls sticking out beneath his wooly hat.

"You'll pay for that, bitch!"

The maniac pulls me up, slams me against a brick building, and covers my mouth. I can smell his rancid breath. He brings the knife up to my face, and my knees buckle. I try to turn away from the steel blade, but he squeezes my jaw between his thumb and fingers and holds me still. Ignoring the fire in my right ankle, I kick at him.

I feel the knife drag across my chest, down my stomach, and stop at my waistband. Please, no. He slides the knife beneath the top of my pants and pulls the knife and pants toward him. I kick at him again, and he clamps my legs still with his own, pressing his hips into me.

He closes his eyes and inhales deeply. "I'm going to enjoy this."

The psycho has every inch of me pinned to the wall. But he will not get Sammy. I keep repeating this over and over. Sammy is smart and savvy. He may only be six, but he's been living on the streets longer than me and knows how to survive. Even though I'm almost seventeen, sometimes I felt like I relied on Sammy, rather than the other way around. I just need to give him more time to get away. I start shaking and twitching. Anything to make it more difficult for this lunatic to finish me off.

"Move away from her!" commands a new voice.

5

Someone else is in the alley. Oh God, another man. I think of what two men can do to me. The freak's hand covering my mouth slackens. I dig my teeth into his fingers.

"Ow, you bitch!" He pulls back his hand. The skin on his face stretches, causing the scars to spread. His eyes widen. He looks inhuman, a monster. "You stupid piece of ...."

He slaps me hard, driving my head up against the bricks. A warm liquid spreads across my face. It has that distinct salty taste of blood as it slides past my lips.

"I said move away from her—*now!*" The other person's voice echoes, filling the alley.

The maniac's still gripping my hands. I push my back against the wall and kick up with my left leg, hitting him in the chest. He stumbles and lets me go. I try to run, my right leg dragging behind me, but he grabs me by my hair and throws me against the wall. I feel the knife plunge into my stomach. The psycho actually stabbed me. My whole body burns. I scream. He stabs me again. I feel myself emptying. There is so much blood. How can it come out so quickly? The inside of my ears feel cloudy, and I can't hear properly. My vision narrows as different pictures flash by. Mostly of my mother.

Strange that I should think of her now. I see her dressed in her pale yellow nightgown, her black hair pulled back in a tight bun, unwilling to help me. Saying that I brought this on myself.

As I feel myself fading away, I realize she is right. I am stupid. I didn't escape anything when I ran away. All I did was leave Navi, my little brother, behind.

I feel a sudden rush of wind, and my legs collapse. I land in a heap on the ground. The searing in my belly lessens as all sensation fades.

With trembling fingers, I wipe the blood from my eyes and blurrily look around. The alley is empty, except for some garbage in a corner. Where did my attacker go? I try to stand, but my legs are too weak. I'm about to drag myself out when a crash shakes the ground. Something smashes onto a pile of discarded boxes, collapsing them. Oh God, it's him. Before I have a chance to react, he's gone again. Something lifts him from the ground and flings him against another wall.

My breath comes in short bursts. I'm sinking in my own pool of blood. There can't be much left inside me. My ears are full and heavy. Every sound around me fades.

Suddenly, I'm pulled from my sinking consciousness and feel myself being lifted away.

"You're safe now. I've got you," a velvety voice says in my ear.

I struggle to lift my eyelids, and I'm looking at the most beautiful face I've ever seen. Seconds before, all that existed was cold and gray. But now the air shimmers. Dazzling bright colors of gold and pink and orange stretch out in front of me.

"Stay with me now," his voice soothes. "You're going to be okay."

I'm looking at an angel, my angel, carrying me off to heaven. No human is this beautiful. His ivory skin is smooth and framed by a short curtain of hair so fair that

7

it radiates light. And his eyes, a shade of blue that only exist somewhere within the secrets of the oceans. I feel a long-forgotten serenity as he carries me away to my final home.

I press my head against his shoulder. His warmth seeps into my skin and heats me to my core. I don't want this feeling to end. I have never felt this safe. I don't know why I ever feared death.

But wait, what about Sammy?

"Where's Sammy?" I whisper.

"Shhh, you're going to be okay," he says.

"No. Where's Sammy? The little boy. He was with me, but he got away before you came."

"He's fine. Everything is fine. Just stay quiet."

"Did you see him? Did he get away? Is he safe?"

He pulls me in closer, so that my face is nestled into his neck. Oh, he smells so good, like warm cinnamon toast.

"He's okay. He's safe."

I relax deeper into his arms. I can leave this life knowing that Sammy's okay.

We soar faster than seems possible. Scenery blurs past. It's hard to breathe. But then I remember—it doesn't matter if I'm breathing. I'm dead.

I must have been a good person when I was alive, contrary to what my mother and Sita always said, to be allowed such a gorgeous angel. I tilt my head so that I can breathe in his scent, and a fiery sensation spreads down my arms and into the tips of my fingers. I have to feel my hand against his skin.

Just as I am about to lay my fingers across his face, we crash through a door.

"Margaret! Margaret!" he shouts.

A crowd gathers around. Hands reach out and touch me. I nuzzle into him as tightly as I can, unwilling to be separated.

"It's okay. They'll help you, fix up your cuts."

I swat away the hands intent on separating me from him. But then I stop. His words penetrate into my brain.

Fix me. I'm not dead? I don't want to be fixed if it means leaving him. I don't want to be fixed if it means going back to the streets. I want to be safe and warm like I was moments ago. I never thought I'd feel that way again.

"No, please don't go," I plead, grabbing onto him.

"I'm not going anywhere. I'll be right here." He gently lays me on a table. The others are moving in between us, probing my eyes with lights. I reach out to him, but my hand is roughly laid back onto the table.

"For God's sake, Ellis, enough of this. She's lost a lot of blood. I need to get her under soon."

A tall slender woman dressed in white rolls me away from him. I feel a sharp prick in my arm, and everything floats away.

TWO

A constant hum whines inside my head. I open my eyes and immediately shut them. The light is blinding. I try again, lifting my eyelids slower this time and squinting for several seconds before my vision adjusts. I'm lying on a cot, with wires and tubes connecting me to a monitor. The room is completely white and windowless. Four concrete walls surround me. There is a counter by the wall across from my bed with cupboards above.

Where am I? The train station? Home? Images force their way through my foggy mind. Dark cold eyes. And blood. So much blood. I push down the covers. My hands hover above my stomach. Trembling, I lower the tips of my fingers onto my abdomen, feeling for a gash, a hole. But there's nothing. Only smooth skin and a tiny bandage the size of a penny. How can that be?

I vaguely remember someone else being there. Someone small? A child? It couldn't be Navi. I press the base of my palms into my forehead, trying to untangle the chaos of images and reassemble them into something that makes sense. There was someone else too. Someone in addition to the child. Someone who helped me. My angel.

"Good, you're awake," says a woman, entering the room.

10

She looks to be my mother's age, but she's nothing like my mother. She is tall and lean and breathtaking. Her pearly hair, which hangs just above her shoulders, glistens. She moves like a dancer and glides toward me in a white lab coat that billows behind her. I struggle to get up, but the room spins.

"Do not be silly. Lie back down." Her delicate hands are surprisingly strong, and she pushes me back onto the bed. "My name is Margaret Turner. You were brought to my clinic last night with cuts to your head and stomach and an injured ankle." She points out the location of my wounds as she speaks. "Though there appeared to be heavy blood loss at first, once you were cleaned up it was clear that the lacerations were fairly minimal. You will be fine. No permanent damage. Your ankle was twisted, so I have wrapped it." She pulls up the covers at the foot of my bed to reveal my right ankle bound in a beige cloth bandage. "You can remove it tonight. It will have healed by then."

She sounds robotic. Despite being immediately drawn to her glorious appearance, I flinch when she touches me.

Margaret peers into my eyes with a tiny light. "Yes, all is good. The surface scarring will heal in a short time. I have something to assist with the process," she says, and turns away to leave.

Her hurried manner of speaking adds to my state of confusion. "Are you a doctor?" I ask, though I assume she must be.

"Yes, I'm a healer."

Healer?

"Please." I reach out and touch the cuff of her white lab coat. "Where am I?"

She looks at me as if I've asked a stupid question and snaps her arm back. "You're in a recovery room, in my clinic."

"And I'm okay?"

"Yes. You are now."

"I don't understand. My ankle snapped. I heard it. Blood was pouring out of me." I sit up and drag my fingers through my hair, stretching my scalp. "It was everywhere. My clothes were soaked in it." My voice is high.

Margaret leans her head to one side and sighs heavily. She reaches above my head and adjusts knobs and buttons on the monitor. Her forehead creases as she furrows her brow and regards me for several seconds before she finally speaks.

"I am a skilled healer, and I repaired all your internal injuries using a technique that leaves a tiny scar." Margaret detaches the wires and tubes from my neck and arms. She returns her gaze to me and smiles stiffly. "Your ankle was not broken. And I have appropriately dealt with that minor injury also. Remove the bandage tonight. You will see that it is fine, and you can walk on it." She glances at the closed door and clears her throat before returning her attention to me. "Now, if that is all, I will return with the medicated cream that will further minimize the scar." Margaret turns to leave.

"Wait," I call out to her, and she stops. She lets out a

great exhalation of air. I press on, despite her clear indication that my exam is over. "You said I was brought here. Who brought me? Was it a man? Was there a child?"

She lets out an almost inaudible gasp, and her hands form into tight balls. When she faces me, her lips have transformed into a narrow, tight line. She moves closer to my bed, and my entire body tenses.

"What exactly do you remember about last night?" Margaret asks, her voice noticeably strained.

"I-I-I don't remember much. It's all fuzzy. Mostly the blood. I remember there was a lot of blood."

"Anything else?" she asks, crossing her arms.

"I remember being lost and in an alleyway." I shift uncomfortably. "I remember a guy dressed in black attacking me, punching me."

"Mmhmm," she says, apparently unmoved.

"I also think there was another guy there. But he wasn't there to hurt me. I think maybe he actually saved me."

"Yes, well, a young man did bring you in here." She pulls her hair back behind her ears and straightens her lab coat. "Anyone else?"

"A little boy?" I say, scrunching up my face.

She places her hands into the pockets of her coat, pulls her shoulders back, and clears her throat. "I will go and check on that. The person who brought you here is just outside. I will be right back." Without waiting for a response, she walks out of the room.

I squeeze my head between my hands. I'm in a clinic. I was messed up badly, but somehow this doctor, healer, as she calls herself, was able to put me back together so well that it's like I was never hurt at all.

But something's not right. This place. That woman. I get off the bed too quickly and grasp the sides of the mattress to steady myself. Where are my clothes? And then I remember what Margaret said. 'He's just outside.' I can't go. He said he would wait for me. I can still feel the warmth as he held me in his arms. I need to see him one more time. Just to make sure he was real.

The door opens. "Well, hello there," says a man, grinning widely as he walks toward me.

But he's not the one who saved me. He's not my angel. This person is all bulk. Bulky body, bulky limbs, and a bulky square face, framed by a mass of red hair. And the eyes, those aren't his eyes. I will never forget those beautiful blue eyes. This guy's eyes are gray.

I scramble back into bed and shield myself under the blankets. I draw my knees into my chest.

"Great, you're awake." He pulls away my covers. Instinctively, I grab them back. "Hey, relax there. I'm not going to hurt you. Just making sure all is healing."

He's dressed in a dark green sweater and faded jeans. I'd have expected a nurse to be wearing a uniform of some sort. His presence makes all my muscles tense. I hold tight to the cover, unwilling to release my grip on the sheet.

"Don't make this difficult," he says. His eyes narrow into slits. He presses his lips into a tight line and wedges his hand beneath the thin blanket. He pushes my knees away and tugs my shirt up.

14

The images I'm trying so hard to keep from surfacing rush through me. I'm pulled back into the alley. I can smell the stale smoke. I can feel myself being held down. And then older memories ambush me. My clothes coming off. Other hands all over me. Groping me. No. Not again.

"Get off me!" I scream, trying to get up from the table. But he continues to bear down into my stomach.

"What is going on?" Margaret is back. She glares at the man pinning me to the bed. "Fallon, I already checked. It is fine," she says, in her halting voice.

"Just making sure." He smiles again, but briefly, as the person behind Margaret steps into view.

It's him. My angel does exist. The sight of him makes me forget to breathe. And then I'm breathing much too quickly. He's really here. He looks exactly as I remember. He isn't much older than me. Maybe just a couple of years. His layers of straight blond hair are cropped close to his neckline and glisten even under the harsh light. He is tall and thin, regal, in his black winter coat and dark blue jeans. His face is round with high cheekbones. His bangs fall to just above his eyebrows. He does look like an angel. And his eyes, so intensely blue, glare at Fallon.

"Take your hands off her!" he barks and charges toward us.

"Ellis, stop!" Margaret grabs for him but misses. Ellis lunges at Fallon, and they crash onto the floor.

"Get a grip," Fallon says, as he effortlessly maneuvers himself on top of Ellis.

"You son of a—"

"Now, Ellis, no need to get Mommy Dearest involved," Fallon taunts.

"Enough of this!" Margaret swiftly walks toward them, bends down, and grabs hold of their collars, jerking them upright.

I lie huddled beneath the sheet as the jumble of fighting and yelling continues around me. I'm so stupid. I should have left when I had the chance. And then as quickly as it started, it stops, and the room grows quiet. Three pairs of eyes turn to me. They study me, as if they'd forgotten I was there.

"Are you okay? Did he hurt you?" Ellis asks, taking a step toward me.

"Of course I didn't hurt her." Fallon makes his way closer to me.

"She was screaming," Ellis says and pulls back on Fallon's shoulder. "I could hear her down the hall. You're frightening her."

I don't move, as a slew of useless escape plans rushes in and out of my mind.

"I'm frightening her? You're the one who stormed in here and launched yourself at me," he accuses, shoving at Ellis with hands that completely cover Ellis's chest.

"Be quiet, both of you," Margaret says. She wrinkles her brow and casts them a menacing look. Still scowling, she turns to me. "I have consulted with Ellis. There was no one else with you, other than the man who attacked you." She nods toward Ellis. "And apparently, he dealt with your attacker, who left the scene."

"That I did," Ellis says, a small smile on his face.

"Yes, well, regardless," Margaret continues, "no one else was there. Certainly not a little boy. Perhaps there was a child in the waiting room when you were brought in, and that is who you are remembering." She stares at me, daring me to disagree. When I don't respond, she simply says, "You are fine to leave now. I will need to do a re-check in a week." She pulls up the collar of her lab coat.

Her tone is absolute, but I can't shake the feeling there's something she's not telling me. My head is muddled, like the replay feature in my brain has broken. I get bits and pieces coming back, but they don't fit together. Parts are missing.

I watch her warily. In spite of the intense confusion and apprehension that consumes me, I can't help but notice how truly lovely she is. Her skin actually shimmers under the cold, bright light.

Margaret moves to the counter opposite the bed and opens one of the drawers. She pulls out a sheet of paper, places it on a clipboard, and hands it to me. I slowly sit up and look at the sheet. It's a questionnaire. Name? Address? Phone Number? Oh crap, now what do I do? No one can know where I am. Or maybe they already do? Have the police been called?

I can't think. The pen shakes in my hand.

"Is there a problem? It is a simple form. Did I not clearly explain why you were brought here? Do you have any more questions about your injuries?"

"Uh, no." I swallow, and my throat feels like it's shrunk.

"Does anyone know I'm here?"

"Like who?" asks Margaret.

Fallon draws up his enormous right hand and scrutinizes his fingernails. He looks like he's assessing the quality of a recent manicure. "I believe she's talking about the police," he states and then locks his gaze with mine. He arches his eyebrows and tilts his head as if he has discovered a secret.

Margaret shakes her head. "I have been rather busy healing your injuries. I did not have time to contact the police." She crosses her arms. She's not offering an excuse, merely stating a fact. "I am a healer, not a doctor. As such, I am under no legal obligation to contact the authorities about your situation. But if you," she flicks her hand at me, "if you would like us to contact someone, including the police, then we will."

"No! I mean, no," I repeat in a calmer tone. "There's no point. You've fixed me, and he's probably long gone."

"Okay then. But I do need that form filled out," she says, pointing to my clipboard.

I look down at the sheet of paper, feeling her eyes on me. My legs twitch nervously beneath the sheet. How am I going to answer the simple yet difficult questions looming on the sheet of paper in front of me? Address? I can't put down train station as my home, even though that's where I spend most nights. And I definitely can't list Weedsport. I can never go back home as long as Sita, my mother's cousin from India, is there. Waiting for me. Waiting to marry me off to some disgusting guy who can't keep his hands off me.

I close my eyes to block out Margaret's glare, but then I'm overcome by an even more disturbing image—Sita's stony face, surrounded by all the men she's forced on me.

I push the tormenting memories back and replace them with Ellis's kind face. I do this over and over, until the awful memories erode and soften. Even before I open my eyes, I am aware of the three faces staring at me. All of them frown.

How long was I gone, reliving the nightmares Sita made me endure?

Margaret studies my face. "I do not have to call the police, but if you are unable or unwilling to provide these simple answers, then ...."

"No, sorry," I stammer. "Just a bit woozy."

I write down the first street name I can think of and continue to make up the rest. I can't take the chance of my family finding me and forcing me to go back. I hand the clipboard back to her, feeling nervous, like when I would hand in a test I was unsure of.

"Thank you," she says, as she scans the sheet.

Her eyebrows pinch together and my stomach drops. Does she know I made it up? Will she call the police? I've got to get out of here.

"Yes, this will suffice," she says, and I breathe a sigh of relief.

Ellis looks at me with concern. "You okay?" he asks, exchanging glances with Margaret.

"Yeah." I shrug. "I'm fine. Ready to go." My skin is covered in gooseflesh, and I rub my hands across my arms.

"You're shivering." Ellis pulls off his coat and places it on top of my blanket.

He rests his hand on top of his coat, and my legs tremble even more despite the sudden warm sensation that fills me.

"Is this normal?" Ellis asks Margaret.

"No, of course it's not normal." Fallon shakes his head in disgust. "It's completely abnormal and pathetic, really, that she trembles in your presence."

"You're an idiot," Ellis says reproachfully to Fallon, and then turns to me, his face gentle again. "Ignore him. Maybe you just need a few more blankets?"

"I will recheck her temperature and circulation." Margaret pulls a thin white tube from her pocket and places it just behind my ear. After a few seconds it beeps, and she pulls it back and twists it between her fingers.

There is a noticeable strain in the room. Even Fallon, who a moment before was smug, looks apprehensive.

"Her temperature is normal." Margaret places the thermometer back into her pocket. "Like I said, I repaired the injuries fully. There should not be any lingering effects," she says, emphasizing the last two words. Fallon's face relaxes. "All is good. Now here is that medicated cream. Apply it to your scar twice a day." She pulls a small tube from her pocket and hands it to me.

Scar? Did she say scar? "I have a scar? On my face?"

"Yes, you have a scar. No, not on your face. That wound I repaired completely. There is a small scar on your stomach. That is why I gave you the cream. Twice a day." Margaret turns and leaves. She stops at the threshold of the door. "Fallon," she calls, without looking at him.

20

Fallon stands rooted to his spot, as if he hadn't heard. His eyes narrow, and he glares at me.

"Fallon," Margaret says, more severely, tapping her fingers on the doorframe.

He jolts, turns away from me, and plods toward the door. His thick, trunk-like arms dangle at his side. Words are muttered between Ellis and Fallon that I can't hear. My breath catches as I realize that Ellis is walking toward the door, away from me.

"Are you leaving as well?" I ask, unable to conceal my disappointment.

"Just so you can get dressed. I'll be waiting right outside the door. Call me when you're ready."

I want him to promise me that he actually will be waiting. I have no idea why it matters so much to me that I get to see him again. After months of living on the streets, I'm used to being alone, taking care of myself. But it was exhausting always being on guard and constantly worrying about my safety. I'm so tired of it. I just want a break. And for some reason, I feel safe with him.

But I stay silent. Even I know that it sounds miserably desperate to ask a complete stranger to be with me. Instead, I stupidly nod and try to get changed as quickly as I can.

I gingerly get out of bed, uneasy about putting weight on my ankle. But it doesn't hurt. I cross the room to the counter, and with each step, place more weight on my right foot, shocked that there is no pain.

I find my clothes neatly piled in the corner. Last night

they'd been drenched in blood. I poke at them, as if the clothes might come alive and blanket me in red slime. I flip up the sides, and when nothing comes at me, I pick them up and turn them in my hands. Someone's really cleaned them.

I'm still feeling a bit wobbly, so the whole process of dressing feels like it takes an eternity. I fumble with my various zippers and buttons, but finally I'm done.

I find a small mirror hanging on the inside of a partially open cupboard. I glance at myself, nervous at what my reflection will look like. I raise my chin and take in the face staring back at me. There are no gaping wounds. In fact, my face looks completely normal. Not a scrape on it. I run a hand across my forehead, cheeks, and neck, amazed by how smooth it feels. I actually look okay. A little thin maybe. My cheeks are slightly drawn, and I am pale. My hair is still a tangled black mess, but at least there's no blood in it. I take a quick whiff under my arms. I smell like a combination of sweat and rubbing alcohol. I clamp my arms tight to my side. I've only been able to clean myself in the bathroom sinks at the train station since I ran away a few months ago. I'm so gross, I can't imagine my time with Ellis will last much longer.

I pull open the door, praying Ellis is on the other side. And he is. I steady myself against the frame. He turns to me and smiles. His eyes sparkle, and his head tilts slightly.

"Great, you're ready," he says, as he grabs onto the door.

His fingers come within inches of my hand. I want to reach out and touch him. I can't remember the last time

I ever wanted to be near a guy, let alone touch him. But then I do remember. It was at a high school dance and I'd been furtively watching Bradley Lawson dance all night, thinking about how lucky those girls were. And then suddenly he came over and asked me to dance. He put his arms around me, and that was it. I couldn't bear it. It felt like being mauled by Sita's men. Poor Bradley. I ran out of the building and never looked back.

Something about Ellis pulls me to him. But I fight my urge and grip the door instead of his hand. My legs wobble as beads of sweat dampen my face.

Ellis steps into the room with me. Before I know it, the door has closed and we are alone.

THREE

I can't believe it. He's actually still here. The air around me has thinned, making it hard to breathe.

"Are you okay?" he asks.

I hold my breath, afraid to exhale. "Yeah, I'm fine. A little dizzy maybe." My voice is high and small.

"Oh, well, here." He slips his arm around me. The instant I feel the weight of his arm against me, I pull away from him. He's blocking the door, so I cross to the other side of the room to create as much distance as I can.

"Sorry." He freezes, his arm suspended in the air. "Did I hurt you?"

"No, you didn't." I force a smile and sit on the edge of the bed.

What's wrong with me? He's not like Sita's disgusting men or the monster in the alley. He's trying to help me.

"I understand your hesitation in calling the police." He walks over and sits down beside me, and this time I don't shrink away. "They most likely won't catch the guy, and it'll just be a pain. But is there someone you want to call? Someone who can come and pick you up? Surely someone will be missing you."

Though his words are meant to be kind, they make

me miserable. No, there is no one. No one cares about me.

I turn and look at him. Even in the stark fluorescent light of the room, he's gorgeous. He watches me, patiently waiting for an answer to what must seem like a simple question. He's sitting so close that if I set my hand down beside me, I'd touch him, but instead I fold my hands on my lap.

I try to think of a reply, other than, 'I only want to be with you.' Even to my ears, it sounds pathetic. Am I so deprived of proper affection and love that I'm willing to latch on to the first person who shows me a tiny bit of compassion? I don't even know him.

I could call Mim. She was my only friend back home. Since leaving, I've tried to call her every few weeks, just to hear the sound of a familiar voice. To feel connected to someone.

I never told her the exact reasons I had to get away, but I think she may have guessed. She was always inviting me to sleep over at her house, and when I eventually divulged my plan to run away, she tried to convince me to live with her and her parents.

I'd been trembling that early August morning when I stepped onto the bus that would start my journey. As the bus lurched forward, I almost screamed out for the driver to stop so that I could go back and accept Mim's offer. Instead I folded my knees into my chest, closed my eyes, and just breathed.

No, I can't call Mim. Not now anyway. Every time I call her, she questions my decision about running away.

And if I told her about Ellis and wanting to stay with him, she'd totally freak. She'd think I was insane. Maybe I am. But he did save me and bring me to this clinic. I look up at Ellis, patiently waiting for me to answer.

"I don't want to call anyone. I feel okay. They'd just worry, you know, if I called them." It sounds like a lie even to me.

"But you've been gone all night. Your family is probably out of their minds. They might have called the police. I think they need to hear that you are okay."

There's no way out of this. I have to tell Ellis the truth. I can't risk him calling the police.

"There's no need to call my family. I'm sure they aren't worried," I say, pained by the truth of my statement. I look down to see my hand clenching the bedsheet.

"What are you talking about? Of course they'd be worried. You're a child, and you've been missing all night!"

"I'm not a child!" His words crush me. He thinks of me as a little kid, nothing else.

"Sorry, I didn't mean anything by it, but you're too young to be out all night."

"I'm not that young. We're probably the same age."

He raises his eyebrows. "Really? How old are you?"

"Old enough to take care of myself."

Even I know how stupid I sound, but I don't like thinking the only reason Ellis is sitting in here with me is that he sees me as a helpless kid.

"And you, how old are you?" I ask, praying the number will end in 'teen.'

He looks taken aback. "I just want to know if you want to call your parents." And then he grins slightly and says, "I'm nineteen."

"Well, I'm almost seventeen!" Definitely not a child, I want to add but don't.

"Okay," he says.

"I'm actually taking a break from my family." I stare into my hands. "They aren't expecting me to call them or anything."

He looks perplexed. It must be the word 'break.' But I won't offer any more. I've already said too much.

After a few moments of uncomfortable silence, he regains his cool composure and says, "Well, is there some other place I can take you?"

The back of my throat feels tight. I can't speak. I can't swallow. Some place he can take me? To do what? We're still sitting on the bed. Suddenly he feels so close to me. Too close. I stand up and take a step away from him.

"Are you okay? You don't look well. I'll go get Margaret." He rises and heads to the door.

What am I doing? I force my breathing to slow down and stretch out my fingers. They had balled into fists.

Maybe he is trying to help me. I take in his face, his kind face, and all the tightness inside me releases. Being with him is certainly safer than being alone.

But why would he want to be around me? He's only offered to take me somewhere, which basically means he'll be dropping me off and then leaving. He has no intention of staying with me. I am nothing to him. I know better than to believe in happy endings. They don't exist for me.

"You don't have to take me anywhere. I'll be fine." My voice catches on the last word.

Ellis is silent. He walks back to me, takes my hand, and leads me away from the exam room. I suppose there is nothing more to say. We'll walk out of this place and go our separate ways.

Tears spill out of the corners of my eyes, and I distract myself by taking in my surroundings. The hallway, just like the exam room, is devoid of color. The walls, floor, and ceiling are all white. It's hard to tell where the floor ends and the walls begin. People mill about, staring in our direction as we pass. Ellis seems unaware of the eyes following us. I guess he's used to people gawking at him. Up ahead I see a large double door made of glass. The exit.

As soon as we step through those doors, he'll be gone. Don't make a scene. Just thank him and walk away. Head held high, shoulders strong. And absolutely no more tears.

As we move outside, I look around but don't recognize anything. A low concrete wall, like the kind that divides highways, surrounds the clinic. Beyond the wall is a road, and beyond that, trees. Lots of trees. We're definitely not in the city anymore. It looks more like the towns near where I live. My insides tumble. Are we close to my home?

"Where are we?" I ask, barely controlling my rising panic. "This doesn't look like one of the hospitals downtown."

"You were hurt pretty badly, and this is a private clinic that was quick to get to."

"But wouldn't it have been quicker to stay in the town?"

His eyes narrow slightly. "Like I said, you looked in bad shape, and I knew Margaret would be able to help." He pauses and runs his hands through his hair, ruffling it up, only to have it all fall perfectly back into place. "I'm not from the city," he continues. "So I thought this would be the best thing to do. Plus it was actually very quick to get here."

"Any place is quick when you can fly," I mumble.

"Sorry?"

"N-nothing. Yeah, so I can just walk back if you could point me in the right direction." The thought of being on my own again sickens me.

"I know Margaret released you from the clinic, but I'm not sure you're ready to walk back to the city. Why don't we get some breakfast and figure out what would be best?"

I grasp onto the twinge of hope. I'm not going back to the streets just yet. I wish I never had to go back. I wish I could feel safe like this all the time, but breakfast is a start.

"Yes, I'd like that," I say.

"My car is parked on the other side of the road. How's your ankle? I can get a wheelchair." His voice is hypnotic. I feel a bit dizzy, but I don't want a wheelchair.

"No, I'm good. My ankle's fine. Amazingly fine."

And as the last word fumbles its way out of my mouth, I trip and almost do a face plant. Instantly, hands are on me, pulling me from within inches of the ground.

"Careful now. Wouldn't want you to get hurt again after all it took to make everything right."

It's Fallon. I didn't even hear him approach, yet here he is, holding me up. I pull away. He smells like bleach. His gray eyes are hollow and look small and out of place in his mammoth head.

"Ellis, if you're not up to the job, I can certainly take over." Fallon smiles, but there is no happiness in his face.

"I've got it," Ellis replies frostily. He takes my hand and leads me across the street.

"What job are you not up ...?" I begin to ask Ellis. But when I turn back, I see Fallon still standing by the doors to the clinic, his eyes fixed on me. "So is that guy a doctor?" I say, trying to sound casual.

The thought of Fallon touching me freaks me out. But instead of answering, Ellis frees his hand from mine. All the warmth I felt vaporizes, and I'm left chilled.

"Okay, here we are," he says.

He opens the passenger door of a black car with tinted windows. I hesitate. What am I doing? And then, out of the corner of my eye, I see Fallon walking toward us. Suddenly all that matters is getting away from him. I quickly climb in and pull the door shut.

Thankfully Ellis gets in before Fallon crosses the street. I go to reach for my seatbelt when Ellis pushes a button, and I'm magically secured beneath a black strap. And we're off.

My fingers dig into my legs. In what seems like a second, we go from a deserted road to one with quite a bit of traffic. I still don't recognize my surroundings. We're moving so fast, I can't see anything clearly. I look at Ellis.

He is the angel who saved me last night. He's not like the others. He's not like the men Sita allowed into my bedroom. He's not like the maniac in the alley. I'm safe with him. How many times will I have to say this to myself before I actually believe it?

Ellis easily negotiates in and out of lanes. It's as if all the other vehicles stand still and he simply weaves around them. Shapes and shades of colors whirl past, all mixed together. The speed is both frightening and exhilarating.

As we drive on, the traffic becomes sparse again. The road narrows into one lane each way. My knees squeeze together as I try to figure out how much time has passed since I saw another car. Maybe one came by, and I missed it.

"Is the restaurant much farther?" I try to keep my voice level, despite the tight feeling in my chest.

"Not much farther at all," says Ellis, his eyes forward.

We slow down a bit, and I'm able to take in my surroundings. All I can see are farmers' fields against a backdrop of trees. No buildings.

"What restaurant is out here?" I ask, staring out my window, wondering if we're moving too fast for me to throw myself out of the car.

"Almost there, almost there," Ellis says, not answering my question at all.

He veers right. We exit the two-lane road and turn onto a one-lane dirt road, flanked by large evergreen trees. We're heading into a forest. Oh my God. What am I doing? He's taking me to some deserted spot to ....

My throat is so dry I can't even swallow. I need to get

out of here. I reach for the handle, only to find nothing there. I push on the door, hoping it will miraculously open.

"You okay? We'll be there in less than a minute."

"Stop the car! Let me out." I bang the door with my fist. It doesn't budge.

"What's the matter?"

It's happening again. I'm alone again with a pervert. And this time, he's going to…. I won't allow it. It can't end like this. I ran away to avoid this. I grab the back of his head and pull so hard that chunks of blond hair fill my hands.

"Ow!" he screams, as the car swerves toward the trees.

My door thrashes against cedar branches, blanketing the windows in greenery. I cross my arms in front of my face, bracing for impact, but the car suddenly lurches back onto the road.

Straightening up, I smack the buttons on the dashboard, and my seatbelt disappears. Nothing is holding me back. I won't let him touch me. This time I will fight. I'll wipe that smug expression off of his face permanently. I'm not weak. I attack every inch of him. His head, his face, his body. I pummel my fists into him. Even the gush of blood streaming out of his nose doesn't deter me.

"Stay away from me! I hate you."

"Kalli, stop!"

The car zigzags, and I lose my balance. Ellis pins me to my seat with one arm and steers the car to the side of the road.

Oh no! We've stopped.

"Get off me!" I yell.

I kick him in the stomach, and he lets go. I slam my body against the door. It won't give. I bash at more buttons and my door flies open. I tumble out, and he grabs onto my shoulder. I shove his arm away and fall to the ground. I fill my hands with gravel and hurry back up. Before I can decide which way to run, Ellis is at my side, his lip swollen and bloody.

"Kalli, what's wrong?"

I fling the stones at him. He shuts his eyes, and I take off running.

"Kalli, come back!" He grabs on to my jacket.

"Let me go!"

"No. Not until you tell me what happened."

"She set this up, didn't she?" I say.

"Who? What are you talking about?" Ellis asks.

"That bitch, Sita."

"Who's Sita?"

He's still holding on. I stop pulling against him. I feel his grip relax just as I had hoped. I can't outrun him, so instead I launch myself at him, head first. We crash to the ground. I sit on top of him and bash my fists all over his body. He shields his face.

"She thinks I'll just take it again. Let another one of her losers touch me. Not this time."

He grabs both my arms, pushes me off, and gets up. "I have no idea what you're talking about. I was just getting you something to eat."

"Do you think I'm an idiot? Is that what she told you?"

33

He shakes his head. "Please Kalli, calm down. I'm sorry I brought you out here."

"Did she promise you an easy hook-up? Say you get to be the first to have your way completely?"

"I would never do that." He wipes the blood off his face with the back of his hand. "You said you wanted to get something to eat. Don't you remember?"

"There's nothing out here. Don't lie to me!" I shove his chest.

"I'm really sorry. I couldn't think of anywhere to go, so I was taking you to my place," Ellis says.

"Your place?" Oh my God! He is going to trap me in his home. Imprison me and torture me. I tear off into the forest. I hear his footsteps closing the gap.

"Kalli, I'm sorry. I didn't mean to scare you. I can take you anywhere you want."

"Get away from me! Leave me alone."

I grab a thick branch from the ground. Brandishing it like a sword, I charge at Ellis. He easily gets away. This time I wield the branch over my head and launch it at him. He ducks behind a tree.

"I've obviously done something to scare you. To make you think I would hurt you. But I would never do that. Nothing bad is going to happen to you. I'm not who you think I am," he says.

"I know exactly what you are and what you want."

"Don't you remember? I found you last night. I only want to help you."

He's messing with me. Trying to confuse me.

"Here, take my phone. Call whomever you want. They can come and get you," Ellis says.

His hand appears from behind the tree, holding out the phone. What's he doing? Does he think I'm that stupid?

"Like there's even a signal out here," I say.

"There is. You can call someone. Anyone. Take it."

"Throw it over," I challenge.

And he does. I grab it and punch in 911. Why aren't they answering?

"Police, ambulance, or fire?" A voice resonates through the phone.

What am I doing? I look up at Ellis. He's leaning against the tree. He looks miserable. His face is bloody and battered, certainly not threatening. He even gave me his phone. If his intention was to kill me, he certainly wouldn't have done that. And the last thing I want is the police. They'd just take me back home. I hang up.

"Look. I'll walk away. Give you all the space you want." He raises his arms in front of him and backs away from me. "You can take my car. Go wherever you want." He tosses the keys and they land by my feet. "I'm so sorry, Kalli. I really only wanted to help you."

I swallow the thick lump at the back of my throat. He gave me his keys. His keys! Who does that? I repeat his words silently. He only wants to help me. Even after I went crazy. Even after I hit him. He's not like the others. What have I done? I fall to the ground, sobbing.

"Kalli? Are you okay? Is something hurting? I don't know what to do to help you. Tell me what you need. Please."

I wish I could disappear. I hear the crunch of his footsteps getting closer. And then I feel the weight of his hand upon my shoulder.

"Kalli?"

"I'm sorry. I don't know what happened," I say.

"You have nothing to apologize for. After what happened to you last night, I never should have brought you out here." He sighs. "Listen, I can take you anywhere you want. Or you can take my car and go wherever you want." He tilts his head and smiles.

"You really live around here?" I ask.

He nods. "We could actually walk. It's that close. But it's fine. We can go somewhere else. Or you could call a cab, Kalli."

I can't look at him. He must think I'm nuts. He's probably hoping I opt for the cab.

"Kalli, what would you like to do?" His voice is so gentle.

I hold out his phone, and he takes it. His fingers lightly touch mine. I don't know what to do. I want to trust him. But I've behaved like a lunatic. He'll think I'm manic. And maybe I am. I've attacked him and accused him of being a pervert.

The feel of his skin against mine makes me feel warm, and the warmth calms me a bit. Suddenly the thought of being inside a home again appeals to me. I miss my house.

"I'd like to have breakfast at your place. If that's still okay with you."

"Absolutely." He gets up and holds his hand out to me.

I take it, feeling a rush of shame.

"I don't know what happened. I'm so sorry. Your face." I've destroyed it. I can't look at him.

He lifts my chin, and I'm forced to acknowledge the damage I inflicted on him.

"It's not your fault," he says. "After all you've been through, I was an idiot to bring you way out here. I wasn't thinking. Kalli, I would never hurt you. I promise."

Ellis opens the car door, and I get in, praying I've done the right thing.

I've barely settled into my seat when we turn left and slow down. We've reached the end of a gravel road and there it is, standing alone—Ellis's house.

It looks quite old. The bricks are crumbling and the paint on the window frames is chipped. There isn't another building in sight. The ground close to the old house is covered in crushed stone. Behind the house is a neglected hay field that ends at a forest of evergreen trees.

I ball my hands and dig them under my legs. I can feel my heart pounding against my ribs. Relax. If he had wanted to hurt me, he's had plenty of opportunity for that.

Ellis gets out of the car, walks around to my side, and pulls my door open. He holds out his hand. I let out a big breath. This is okay. Comforting myself that I can leave whenever I want, I take his hand.

The gravel crunches beneath my feet. I close my eyes and take in the sound. I'm suddenly a small child, holding my dad's hand as we walk up our driveway. My feet grind in the tiny stones, massaging my soles through my shoes. And then another image materializes. This time it is my hand that encases a smaller one. Could it be Navi that I keep seeing? It has to be my little brother. I don't know any other child. But as quickly as the picture comes, it melts away.

"Kalli, you okay?" Ellis asks.

"Yeah, fine," I say, shrugging myself free of the memory.

We are standing in front of his door. It's made of solid steel. Nothing can break in or out.

"Here we are." The feel of his warm, sweet breath against my skin calms the hairs standing on the back of my neck, and his soothing voice unclenches my stomach. Ignoring my tangled thoughts, I move through the open door.

FOUR

"Ooh," I gasp. A scent of fresh pine and cinnamon wafts throughout Ellis's home. It smells like him, and I love it immediately. Wide wooden planks cover the floors. There are several brightly colored sofas and armchairs placed throughout, and many large, tree-like plants grow from enormous clay pots. I've never seen anything like them. The leaves sparkle. Tiny yellow flowers hang like pendants from the branches. The ceiling, a crisscross of thick timber, is so high the trees have grown to great heights despite being indoors. The walls are entirely concealed by books. Thousands of books. It's positively the most brilliant place I've ever set my eyes on.

"This is amazing."

"Thank you," he says, looking amused.

He removes his coat and neatly places it on a rack. He helps me out of mine and drops it onto one of the hooks.

"Have a seat. I'll be right back."

I watch him walk away and disappear behind a door. What am I doing? I can't stay here. A tiny whimper escapes my lips. I squeeze my head between my hands. Think. Think. I have to get out of here. I'm almost out the door when I hear him.

"Hey? What are you doing?" Ellis asks.

My legs are jumpy, ready to flee.

"Is everything okay?" He touches my back, and I whip around. "Sorry, I didn't mean to startle you." He immediately steps away, his eyes wide.

His face is damp. The blood has been washed away, but his lip is puffy. Guilt knots up my stomach.

"It's okay if you want to leave. I can take you anywhere you want," Ellis says again.

I let out a slow breath. There's something about him that makes me want to trust him. Plus it's so warm in here. I don't want to go back to being cold and alone again.

I shake my head. "No. I'm fine."

"Are you tired? You can rest before we eat or go wash up in the bathroom."

There is kindness in his eyes. My head swims. I need a moment to figure out what to do. I can't think straight when I'm so close to him.

"The bathroom would be great," I say, as calmly as I can.

"It's at the back, through the red door."

He holds out his hand, and I take it. We walk past the enormous potted trees, toward the kitchen area. There's a large island with a multicolored, tiled countertop. I run my fingers against it as we pass by. It feels wonderfully cool and soothes me.

Beyond the kitchen is an immense bed, covered in a checkered purple and red duvet. Oh no. I have to get out of here. I'm so gullible. He lied. He is going to ....

But we walk right past the bed. Ellis's pace never even slows down. And I breathe again.

"Here you go. There are clean towels and soap on the shelves. If you need anything, just ask." He opens the door to the bathroom.

I suddenly remember my backpack. It holds all my possessions, the few that there are. Some clean clothes, my toothbrush, and the remains of all the money I had stashed away since deciding to leave home. It also has a few smaller items that are full of important memories. I must have dropped it in the alley. Ellis studies my face.

"Is everything okay?" he asks.

"My backpack. I must have left it—"

"No, it's just in the car." He walks out the front door.

I look around. Is that the only way out? Before my mind can unravel with images of my doom, he returns holding my well-worn backpack.

"H-how?"

"I grabbed it when I grabbed you last night. Figured it was important."

"But I didn't see it in the car."

"You were a little distracted." He smiles.

I take the bag, step into the bathroom, close the door, and sink to the floor, my legs shaky and my face burning. When my breathing finally slows, I stand up and look around. There's no window. No way for me to escape. But it's okay. I don't need to escape. I squeeze my eyes shut with the base of my palms. Please let something good be happening in my life, I pray, hoping that someone out there will finally grant me a wish. I rest my hands on the counter and open my eyes. I thought I knew what I was doing when I left home. I thought anything would be better than the horrors I faced in my own house. But it's been so hard, and I'm so tired. I'll just rest for a bit, and then I'll leave.

Unlike the main room, the bathroom is startlingly bland but still amazing. Sparkling white sink, big soaker tub, and a shower with so many faucets, that if they were all on, I'd be propelled right out of it.

I search through my bag for my toothbrush and some clothes. I pull out a pair of jeans, a scraggly sweater, and some underwear, and set them on the bench. I find some toothpaste in a drawer and scrub my teeth along with the entire inside of my mouth.

Despite the door being firmly shut, I hesitate to undress. I'm not sure if it's his eyes or my own that I'm hiding from. There is a long mirror hanging on the wall, and I don't want to see what my body has transformed into.

I take a nervous glance at myself in the mirror and immediately wish I hadn't. In just over three months, my body has sunken in on itself. Angular bones protrude under my skin. The long, lean muscles that once shaped my arms and legs have vanished. I look dull and unhealthy. I was never as dark-skinned as my mother, but now I just look sickly pale. The only thing I inherited from her was my thick black wad of hair. The color of my eyes and paler skin I got from my dad.

It was almost a daily event to hear Sita saying that the

only thing that should be green is money. She'd say this, staring directly into my moss-colored eyes. I know the fair color of my skin also annoyed her.

The other thing that shocks me is the sliver of a mark below my belly button. It's so strange. How did Margaret heal me up so well? There are no bloodied bandages to change. I don't have any pain. Maybe it hadn't been so bad. I once read that wounds to the head bleed a lot. Perhaps that's true for cuts to the stomach as well.

As I step into the shower, I cringe, worried that the water will sting the wound. But it doesn't. It passes over me and my weariness begins to release and wash away.

I could never relax like this at home. I was always on guard, wondering when Sita would produce the next despicable marriage candidate. Terrified that he'd be the one to commit the vilest act. To violate me completely. They didn't care that I was so much younger than they were.

I rest my hands against the wall. Ellis is not like those guys. He has been nothing but kind and attentive. I totally freaked out in the car. He even gave me his phone, offered me his car. I could have called anyone or driven away. I can trust him. I can.

I lather up the bodywash and scour my skin, head to toe. My flesh stings but I keep going.

Finally I am red and raw and clean. I close my eyes and wish I had something comfy and soft to change into. I don't want to wear the crispy old jeans and scratchy sweater.

Within seconds of my wishing it, he appears, or rather

his arm appears, laden with a pile of plushy soft fabrics.

"I thought you might find these comfortable." With his head concealed behind the door, he expertly tosses the clothes onto the bench.

I instinctively cover the parts of me that should be covered, but he is already gone.

I open the bathroom door and there he is, arms crossed, leaning against the back of the kitchen island. He's wearing a gray T-shirt and a pair of jeans. The clothes fit him so well that I am momentarily drawn away from his face to his perfect body.

"Feel better?" he asks.

"Yes and, um, thank you for the clothes."

I am grateful for them. The softness of the fabric melts against my skin. I only wish I wasn't wearing such a shapeless outfit. His clothes mold so closely against his body. Lucky clothes.

"They look great on you." Again his timing is flawless. Either he is reading my mind, or he's uncannily sensitive to my every need.

I stand there awkwardly, as his eyes sweep over me. They are such a deep blue color, almost black. It's hard to breathe when I look at them.

"Are you hungry?" He motions to the platters of food laid out on the kitchen counter.

There is a heaping basket of thickly sliced bread,

cheese, fresh fruit, and tall glasses of juice. My stomach grumbles loudly as if it just woke up from a deep sleep. I am so hungry, so completely and overwhelmingly hungry. These past months, food and the pursuit of it have been one of my main driving forces. And now here it is, all laid out for me.

I eat until my stomach finally fills. Actually overfills. I feel the food trying to come back up. I close my eyes, unwilling to relinquish my hold on this meal. I will not throw up. I will not throw up in front of Ellis. Just breathe.

"Sorry, I didn't leave any for you," I say.

"Don't worry about it. Would you like something else?"

Why didn't he eat? Did he put something in the food? Stop it. I should be grateful. My paranoia has no limits.

"No, I'm good." I steady myself against the counter and wipe the clammy sweat that beads on my forehead. "Maybe a glass of water," I add.

Something soft rubs against my leg. It's a cat—actually two cats. They're circling the kitchen, looking for remnants of food that have fallen to the floor.

"You okay with cats?" he asks.

"I love them." I reach down to stroke the fur of a gray tabby.

As my fingers move across the cat's silky back, I am thrown into a memory of my thirteenth birthday and my parents, bubbling with smiles, handing me a box with holes in it. From inside came the tiniest of squeals. I still remember that shaking, excited feeling I had as I opened the box and set my eyes on a fluffy orange and black kitten. I held her little body against my face and knew I would love her forever. Sadly, forever didn't last.

When I was fourteen, I became an older sister. A year later, Sita, moved in from India, to help take care of the baby. Immediately upon setting her big boney feet into our home, she declared that my cat Kasha was a danger to the new baby and must be gotten rid of. Despite my desperate pleas and promises to keep Kasha away from the baby, my mother sent her to the Humane Society.

I called about her every day. She wasn't eating or drinking. The woman at the society tried to reassure me that it would take time for Kasha to adjust to her new surroundings, and she would be fine. I knew she wasn't fine. Her heart was broken just like mine, and after two agonizing months of calling, I was told that she had taken a turn for the worse one night and died.

I remember that moment as if I was standing holding the phone right now. I hated my mother and Sita. I hated Sita for destroying the one thing I loved more than anything, and I hated my mother for letting her. As I hung up the phone, I thought that I should just run away. I wish I had. If only I had known what was to come.

I don't realize I'm crying until I see the drops fall onto the cat.

"You okay?" Ellis's voice brings me back.

I quickly wipe away the wetness. "Must be a bit tired." I smile weakly.

"You go and relax. I'll feed Bo and Lucy and be right over."

46

He fills up two little metal bowls with some dry kibble. Bo and Lucy stand on hind legs, reaching up for the food.

When he's done, Ellis comes and sits down beside me. His leg brushes against mine.

"Are you feeling okay?" he asks.

The sound of his voice is gentle and melodic, like listening to a love song. My breathing speeds up. I am behaving like those brainless girls at school who drool over anything male. I want to be better than that, but it's hard when he's sitting so close to me.

I have no idea why he makes me feel like this. Yes, he's good looking, but it's more than that. I'm drawn to him even though I don't really know him. I've obviously been alone for so long that I've forgotten how to normally interact with people.

"Kalli? You okay?" he repeats.

"Yeah, I am. Your place is amazing. It's so colorful, like living in a rainbow."

It's such an effort to make conversation when all I want to do is look at him. His lips curve at the corners. The swelling has already gone down.

"It's a bit much, but I like it. The home I grew up in was very bleak. I hated it. So I went a bit wild with my own place."

I don't want to keep staring at him, so I look around for something else to talk about.

"Those trees. How do they grow so tall inside?"

"Ah, yes. Another thing we didn't have much of when I was growing up, plants. I found these in a nursery up north. I can't remember what they're called, but Lucy and Bo love to climb them." He sinks back into the sofa. "Do you like to read, Kalli?"

"Yes, I do," I answer truthfully.

One of my escapes from Sita used to be to hide out in the local library and lose myself in one story after another. When I left home, I took only one book with me, my favorite, *Dr. Dolittle*. My dad used to read it to me when I was little.

Suddenly, Ellis is up on his feet, with his hand held out to me. Our fingers touch and sparks shoot through me. He leads me to one wall of books. Few look familiar. Some don't even seem to be written in English.

"How many languages do you know?"

He smiles, and my bones turn to mush.

"I know a few," he answers casually.

A dream come true. Smart and handsome.

"Well, please feel free to choose any book you like."

His tone is polite but uncertain, magnifying the fact that despite my weirdly intense attraction for Ellis, we're still just strangers.

"Well, maybe later," he says.

I look at him puzzled.

"The books. Maybe you can pick one later."

"Oh yeah, later. Thanks."

Later. I'll be here later? That's a good sign. I'm in no hurry to go back to the streets.

His face is no longer smiling. He looks wistful, as if he can sense the battle raging within my head.

"How's your cut?" He motions to my stomach.

I stare at him. Can he see right through me?

"It's fine. It doesn't even hurt," I say. "It's kind of weird though. I remember when I was in the alley and seeing all that blood coming out of me. There was so much. But in the shower …." I hesitate. "I, ah, looked at the cut on my stomach and it's so small. And a tiny scar was already there. When I was younger, I fell off my bike. I had this huge gash in my leg and had to get stitches. It looked awful for a long time. Like some centipede erupting from beneath my skin." I wince at the memory. "And these wounds were way deeper than when I fell off my bike. I just don't get how it all healed so fast. I mean it doesn't even hurt. Kind of like it never happened."

"Did you ask Margaret about it?"

I shrug. He angles his head and raises his eyebrows, encouraging me to go on. When I don't, he says. "Ah, yes, her explanation probably wasn't very helpful. Sometimes it can be difficult to push Margaret for more. She comes across as unapproachable, but she is an excellent healer."

"Healer? Yeah, that's what she called herself," I say, running my fingers over the spines of the books. "So she's not a doctor?"

"She knows traditional medicine, so, yeah, she's a doctor." He leans his arm against the bookshelf. "But she's also trained in advanced healing techniques and thinks of herself as better than a doctor. She believes she can heal almost anything." He pauses and mimics me by moving his fingers across the books, until our fingers are inches apart. "But anyway, next time you see Margaret, you should ask her. She loves talking about her advanced training and her own brilliance."

"You know her really well?

"I know her pretty well," he says.

"Did you say next time? Why would I see Margaret again?" My chest tightens, and my fingernails dig into the supple books.

"Isn't that what she said back at the clinic? That you'd need to be checked again?"

She did, but I have no intention of going back.

We stand in silence for a while. Ellis seems tense and on guard. He continues to move his hands over the books. Why does it matter to him if I go back or not? I don't like the awkward quiet, and I feel compelled to say something. My cheeks redden. I search the room, hoping for some inspiration to help me say something brilliant, to redirect the conversation.

He is still looking at me, his radiant eyes unblinking. I wish I could completely trust him and allow myself to let go of all the fears and doubts. I feel like I'm shrinking. Terrified everything I need to believe about Ellis will vanish. I want someone to exist who actually cares about me, and I want that person to be Ellis. I've been looking after myself for so long. Even when I was at home, no one gave a thought about my well-being. I want a break. Just a tiny break. I know I should be strong and independent, but I can't remember the last time I felt taken care of, and I want to feel that way for a bit longer.

I look at him, searching his face for some sign of wickedness. His eyes are still fixed on me, waiting for me to speak.

"Why did you help me?" I ask. "You don't even know me."

"Um, okay." He looks taken aback. He moves to the sofa, and I follow him, my fingers tapping nervously on the sides of my legs as I pad along behind him.

"I found you in an alley being beaten. I wasn't going to just walk away." He sounds agitated, but his face remains calm.

"It's just that not everyone would risk getting involved in someone else's problem."

His expression softens. "Well, they should. I can't imagine anyone not wanting to help you."

My life has hardened me. I have been made to believe that goodness is finite, but maybe for some it is infinite.

He looks sincere. His eyes are pulling me in, yanking at my heart to believe he is good. He even stood by me when I flipped out in the car. Plus he has cats. He likes them. He takes care of them. I can trust him.

FIVE

It's starting to get dark outside. I can't believe I've spent the entire day with Ellis. I'm sitting in an armchair, pretending to read a book. My eyes skim over the pages. My thoughts scatter, and I'm unable to link the words to form a meaningful sentence. Ellis has stepped outside to retrieve something from his car. I give up my pretense of reading and wander around. It's just one big room, and there's only one way out. The walls feel like they are closing in on me. Imprisoning me. Talking with Ellis earlier today eased my worries. There's something about him, a quality he possesses, that makes me believe in him. Like when he holds my hand. Instead of freezing up, as I normally did whenever a guy touched me, I feel calm. But in his absence, my worries, which I thought I had reconciled, return. It's as if I only feel okay about this situation when Ellis is physically present. Why have I become so fickle? My belief in his character constantly wavers. I move to the window and pull back the curtains, expecting to see Ellis charging back to the house, armed with some weapon to harm me. But instead, I see him leaning against his car, a phone pressed to his ear.

I tug up at the window. It's painted shut. His head

turns to the house, and I duck behind the curtain. Did he see me? I rush back to the sofa, my throat dry. Even though I am staring at the door, expecting his arrival, I gasp when he returns.

"Sorry, didn't mean to startle you."

"You didn't," I lie. I lean back into the sofa. "You know, I don't think I ever thanked you for saving my life. How does one thank someone for that?"

"Well, you're very welcome. I'm glad I was there to help." He appraises me skeptically. "Kalli, we don't have to talk about it if you don't want to, but I was just wondering about, you know, 'the break' you're taking from your family. Has it been a long time?"

My stomach tightens, and I grind my fingernails into my palms.

"Um." I have no idea how to respond. Delving into my home life and the reasons I left are not my favorite topics. I clasp my hands around my knees, making myself smaller.

"Don't worry about it. I shouldn't have asked," he apologizes.

"No, it's okay. I just haven't talked about it with anyone other than Mim."

"Mim?"

"Yeah, she's a friend," I say, fidgeting with my hands.

He holds my hands between his, quieting my fingers. "Kalli, it's really okay. You don't have to tell me anything you don't want to." But the cuts on his face say the opposite.

"I'm really sorry about your face" I say.

"Don't even think about it. Considering what you must

have been going through—what I put you through—this is nothing. It makes me so angry to think of anyone hurting women. Of hurting you."

One of the cats rubs up against his legs, and he immediately scoops it up.

"Some people are sick." Ellis holds the cat close to his chest, and the air fills with the rumble of purring. "Several months ago, I was driving, and I saw this guy beating a bag with a stick. I don't know why, but I pulled over. As soon as I got out, he took off." He shakes his head. "Gutless ass. Getting his kicks by bludgeoning two kittens."

"That's terrible," is all I can manage to say.

He smiles. "But they're okay now. Aren't you, Lucy?" He plops the cat down between us, and she immediately nestles in his lap.

Isn't there a saying about judging people based on the way they treat animals? Ellis is so kind and gentle with Lucy. He must be a good person. He shifts and our legs touch. I suddenly feel so warm and relaxed. Lucy trusts him and so can I. Decent men do exist. I've just never had the good fortune of knowing any, until now.

And before I change my mind, I turn to Ellis. "Actually, I would like to tell you about why I left home."

I lock my gaze with his glorious eyes. Yes, it will be better to tell him, at least some of it. I need to be careful so that he doesn't think I'm weak. I won't be his charity case. I won't be anyone's charity case. I take a deep breath and let my shoulders relax.

"I left home a few months ago, just before school

started," I begin. "Things got complicated at home after my dad moved out over a year ago."

"Your father left you?" he asks.

"Yeah, he's a mechanic, and he heard about some great opportunity to relocate to Pittsburgh and open up a chain of car repair shops."

"Do you still see him? Do you know where he is?" Ellis asks.

I nod. "I know where he is, but I haven't seen him for a long time."

I think about the last time I saw my dad. I had been so sure he would rescue me from Sita and the men she insisted I allow into my bedroom. But of course, he didn't.

Tears sting the corners of my eyes. I pretend to brush back hair from my forehead and wipe them away before Ellis sees.

"Anyway, Sita, my mother's cousin from India, also lives at my house, and she and I didn't get along."

My hands shake. I'm not ready to share this part of my past. I steady my palms, hoping Ellis hasn't noticed. It is getting difficult to hide my emotions. Talking about it is like reliving it. I need to stop.

"So I needed a break. And at the end of the summer, I simply left," I say.

He looks shocked. He doesn't understand. How could he? I'm such a fool to believe that he would see me as brave. I didn't tell it properly.

Pangs of sadness tear into me. I've ruined this. I haven't come off strong and independent. I've come off sad and angry and worthless. I'll be back out on the streets. All my hopes disappear like an interrupted dream.

"I'm so sorry, Kalli."

I shrug.

He looks at me as if I'm another stray that he's ended up with. I'm such an idiot. I don't want his pity. I figure it's better if I initiate the goodbye than if he does it. At least this way, I retain some dignity.

"Well, thanks for everything," I say in an unnaturally high voice, staggering to my feet.

"What? You're leaving?"

"Yeah. I should go. Should let you get to ... well, whatever." I laugh nervously.

"No. You don't have to go. Margaret's great and all, but you were hurt badly. Why don't you just lie down for a while, and then we can decide what to do."

"You still want me to stay?"

He stands up and brushes a strand of hair from my face. "Yes, I still want you to stay."

"Well, I guess I'm feeling a bit tired." I rub my eyes.

"Okay, I'll show you where you can rest." He starts to get up but then suddenly freezes. His face tenses.

"Ellis?"

Nothing.

"Ellis?" It comes out like a squeak, but this time he turns and looks at me.

"Right, let's go." His words come out in a burst, and his mouth is tight.

He grabs my arm and roughly ushers me along. I pull

back from the unexpected pain.

"Sorry, Kalli. You go and get some rest. I just need to take care of something."

Take care of something? Now? I stand rooted to the spot.

There's a loud bang on the front door. Ellis looks strained and my muscles tense in response.

"Kalli, it's fine. Go lie down. I'll deal with this and be right back."

And then it finally makes sense. The phone call he made outside by his car. He was calling his girlfriend. Now she's on the other side of the door. How can I have been so stupid to even think that he could ever care about me like that? He's shown no indication of any feelings other than worry for my well-being. He likes to help. He helped me just like he helped the cats. Nothing more.

"You know, actually, I'm going to get going." I move as quickly as I can to retrieve my backpack. I blink away the tears that threaten to fall onto my cheeks. I won't let him see me cry.

"Did you say you were going somewhere? I don't think so," says a familiar voice.

My hands immediately clench. I turn, and blocking the entire doorway, is Fallon.

SIX

Though my contact with Fallon has been minimal, seeing him blocking the door fills me with panic. Fallon looks like a mammoth. His body is taking up more than its fair share of space.

"Get out, Fallon." Ellis crosses in front of Fallon to prevent him from getting farther inside.

"I'm not going anywhere. Looks like I got here just in time," he says, and shoves Ellis aside. He steps toward me. "Did I hear you say you're leaving?"

My legs won't move. They feel heavy like something is holding them from beneath the floor.

"Fallon, what do you think you're doing?" Ellis demands.

"A house call. Isn't that nice of me?" Fallon spits out each word.

"It's all fine." Ellis's lips are barely moving.

"Oh, really? Have you seen yourself in a mirror lately? It doesn't look like everything is fine to me." Fallon moves closer.

Ellis grabs him, struggling to hold him back. I am dumb with fear. Frozen to the spot. No. I won't be a victim again. I search the room, my eyes wide. There has to be another way out.

Fallon easily pulls away from Ellis and edges closer toward me. The hairs on my neck stand straight up. My breath comes up in shallow bursts. I head for the bathroom. A closed door is better than nothing. I'm only a couple of feet from the threshold when I hear Margaret's voice.

"This is ridiculous. Ellis, move aside. I don't have time for this nonsense."

"This wasn't expected, Margaret. I didn't know you were coming," Ellis says.

"Well, I am here now, and I need to check Kalli's stomach and make sure it is healing as it should be."

"You said she should come back in a week. It hasn't even been a day."

"I am perfectly aware of how much time has passed. I certainly hope you are not questioning my judgment, Ellis." The sound of her staccato voice tightens my stomach into a hard ball. I'm practically inside the bathroom.

"Kalli?" Margaret calls out to me.

I stand frozen, fingers touching the doorknob.

"Kalli," she commands.

I have no choice. I turn and face her.

"It's fine." My throat is thick, and my words are lost inside. I swallow, but my throat still feels blocked. "My stomach is fine," I say a bit louder.

She glares at me, her face frosty.

"I believe I am more capable at drawing such a conclusion." Margaret sounds annoyed. "I do not have much time," she continues. "Come here and let me have a look. If that wound gets infected, it will spread throughout your entire body. Is that what you want?"

"Did you discover a problem after we left? Did something abnormal show up on a scan or X-ray?" Ellis asks.

Margaret exhales deliberately. "Yes, there was something I noticed while reviewing one of the diagnostic tests I performed."

My heart rate quickens. She found something?

Ellis walks over and takes my hand. The instant I feel his skin against mine, a warm calm spreads inside me.

"It's better to make sure you're okay." He leads me back to the sofa.

"Ellis, honestly," Margaret says irritably, as she walks to the sofa. "We need to move this along. Kalli, come here, and I will have a look."

We walk by Fallon, who is still crowding the door. I'm not sure how exposed I am going to be when Margaret examines me, and I certainly don't like the idea of Fallon being so close. I lie on the sofa, still holding onto Ellis's hand. Margaret shakes her head. She obviously thinks I'm being silly, but I don't care. The feel of my fingers intertwined with his is the only thing that keeps me from bolting onto the street.

Margaret pulls up my shirt, thankfully revealing very little of my body. The exam is quick. She feels my stomach with her hands and then uses an instrument that resembles a paint roller on one end and a funnel on the other. As the roller paves across my abdomen, Margaret looks into the funnel.

"Yes, everything is proceeding as it should be. Just make sure you keep putting on the cream to prevent any infection,"

Margaret says briskly. She bends over and places her instruments into a black bag. "What happened to your face, Ellis?" She gets to her feet, pulling the bag over her shoulder.

"Nothing. Bumped up against something. Wasn't watching where I was going," he says, covering the side of his mouth with the back of his hand.

"Well, I suggest you be more careful." Her eyes linger on Ellis and then she turns to me. "I will need to see you for a follow-up in a week."

"Another follow-up? I really appreciate your concern and that you actually came out to see me, but I can just go see my own doctor."

Her eyes narrow. "Can you really?"

"Yes, of course," I say, sitting up, still holding Ellis's hand.

She laughs and then stops abruptly. "Kalli, stop playing this game."

"Margaret, what are you doing?" Ellis says, his voice higher than usual. His fingers tense around mine.

"I agree with Margaret. Let's stop playing this game and move on to a better one." Fallon smiles.

"Fallon, get out!" Ellis yells.

Margaret carries on as if there hasn't been an interruption. "Now we all know that the information you filled out on the chart at the hospital was false. The address and phone number are completely fictitious." She pauses and stares at me accusingly.

My mouth is dry.

"As I said," she continues, "I am not legally bound to

report you to the authorities, but I do feel a moral obligation to make sure your wound heals properly, and if you are not going to let me follow up, then ...?" She glares at me, as if she is challenging me to call her on her threat.

"Margaret! Stop it. What are you doing?" Ellis demands.

I am a fool. I look at him, shocked and hurt. I yank my hand free from his. "You told her?"

"No. Of course I didn't." Ellis glares at Margaret.

Margaret looks amused as she nudges him out of the way and puts herself beside me.

"You think we need Ellis to tell us about you?" Margaret asks. "We check all information that patients provide when we enter it into our system, and yours was invalid. Once you entered my clinic, you became my patient, and I am obligated to provide you with the best medical care I can. So you can either allow me to provide this personally, or I can call the necessary authorities and let them see to your care."

I'm trapped. She knows I've left home. Of course she knows. Who else would go to a free clinic? People who can't afford to pay. Runaways. Me. I can't let her call the police. I can't go back home.

My legs tremble as I try to figure my way out of this. She said one week. I can disappear in less than a week.

"Okay, I'll come back to your clinic to get rechecked," I lie.

I feel her icy eyes boring into me, like she's trying to figure out if I am lying.

"Good. I thought you would see that was the best way

to go," she says, with a note of warning in her voice. "And, in the mean time, you will remain here with Ellis. I am sure that is agreeable to you." She crosses her arms looking smug.

What did Margaret just say? She's telling me that I have to stay with Ellis? It's not her decision. I look up at him. Of course staying here would be amazing. A week of warmth. A week of sleeping on something soft. A week of delicious meals. I could rest and regain my strength.

And having a little more time with Ellis, well, that would be.... But I could never ask this of him.

"No, that's not fair to Ellis. I'll come back to your clinic, I promise."

"There is no choice here, Kalli," she scolds. "If I can't be certain that you will be properly taken care of and that you will be coming for a follow-up, I will have to call the police." She brushes past Ellis toward the front door. A cat's meow momentarily pulls away her attention, but she quickly regains her train of thought. "It would be irresponsible of me to do anything else."

"You're right. It's not fair to ask Ellis," Fallon says. "You'll stay with me. I'll keep a very close eye on you." He crosses his enormous arms across his chest, as mine fall limp by my side.

"It looks like you do have a choice after all. Ellis or Fallon. You pick," Margaret says.

I want to scream. This isn't right. Margaret has no right to make me choose. Going with Fallon is no different than going back home. Either way, I'd rather be dead. But Ellis? A part of me still believes he is my angel, and even though I know it's too much to hope for, I do want to stay with him. But why would he want me? He doesn't even know me. Everyone who was supposed to protect me didn't. Why should he be the exception? I search his eyes hoping to find the answer. And I do, when he speaks.

"Kalli, I'd like you stay here with me." Ellis reaches down and takes my hand again, grounding me with the warmth of his touch. "I'll take you to the clinic in a week. I want to help. It's important to make sure you're okay."

His hand surrounds mine, and I don't pull away. It's not threatening. It's protective. He is the exception.

"Thank you. I'll stay."

Fallon mutters under his breath.

"All right, now that that is settled, I will see you in one week," Margaret says sharply.

Before she leaves, she restates the importance of the medicated cream. Fallon doesn't move. He simply stands by the door, arms crossed, staring at me. His eyes bore into my stomach.

"We're done, Fallon. Time for you to go." Ellis holds the door open.

"Are you sure you can handle this, Ellis? Considering your last mess-up, I think I better hang around and help."

"We don't need your help."

They stare at each other, neither one wavering.

"Fallon!" Margaret orders from outside.

"Don't worry, Kalli. I'll make sure you heal up just right," Fallon hisses and then turns, slamming the door shut behind him.

SEVEN

Within seconds of Margaret and Fallon leaving, my muscles ease and my fingers loosen.

"Are you okay?" Ellis locks the front door.

"Yeah, I'm okay."

"I had no idea that was part of the treatment. I'm really sorry," he says.

I shake out my arms and legs, and stand up. I don't want to spend any more time talking about Margaret and Fallon. I've already decided I'll never let them near me again. I have one week to sort it all out.

I peer out of the window and notice the darkening sky. But inside, the room is washed in a lovely warm light. It looks almost as bright as when I arrived this morning, when the sun streamed in through the windows. I search the room for the source of light. I can't see any lamps. And then I see them. Hundreds and hundreds of tiny little white lights illuminate the giant tree-like plants. They shimmer like Christmas trees.

They're magical and scatter my thoughts for just a second to a happy memory of being wrapped in my mother's arms. My dad had his arm around her shoulder, and the three of us moved like one, taking in the Christmas display of a field of pine trees glistening with lights. I wrap my arms around myself, trying to recreate the feeling of being loved and safe.

"You cold?" Ellis asks. He grabs a soft, fluffy blanket from one of the sofas and lays it on my shoulders. "It must be close to dinnertime. Do you want to eat in or go out?"

His question dispels my doubts. If he wanted to hurt me, he would never give me this choice.

"Stay in," I say, because I'll be back outside in the cold soon enough.

He has ready-made pizza dough in the fridge, which we layer with cheese and vegetables. Ellis warms some fresh rolls, and I help make a salad. He's set places by the stools at the kitchen island, and I'm ecstatic that the placement of the stools allows our knees to graze.

This time I force myself to eat at an acceptable pace. I learned from my earlier overindulgence that my shrunken stomach needs to be treated delicately. I take tiny bites of the pizza and swallow each piece completely before taking another.

It's a challenge to exercise such self-control. But my spirits are soaring. I can't believe I am sitting next to the most heavenly looking person, eating deliciously warm food, with the prospects of existing like this for another week. It's a dramatic change to where I'd been just twenty-four hours earlier.

I find out a few details about his life. His family lives out west. He moved here after high school and started a business selling stuff that he's made. Ellis lights up when he talks about the inventions he's working on, making him even more gorgeous. His car is the main thing. I kind of fade out when he goes into details about changing this and adding that. I get lost in the color of his eyes. I don't want him to think I'm not interested in what he's saying, so I ask him if I can see some of the stuff he's made. Considering how excited he was talking about it, I expect him to agree instantly, but he looks taken aback.

"Yeah, sure. They're in my workshop, so maybe later. It's really late. You should get some rest," he says, while we're clearing up the dishes. "Margaret is brilliant, but you have been through a lot, and you shouldn't get overtired."

We pile everything into the dishwasher, and then I help him refill the cats' bowls. I go into the bathroom to get ready and remember I don't have any proper pajamas. I only packed a small backpack when I left home, a couple of changes of clothes, a towel, a blanket, my book, all the cash I had saved, and a photo of my little brother, Navi.

My heart clenches in a pang of guilt. Navi. From the second my dad placed him in my arms, I was hooked. He was so tiny. My parents were busy with their jobs so his care fell to me whenever I wasn't at school.

Sita tried to take over his care when she barged her way into our lives. But even she couldn't break our bond.

As soon as I got home from school, Navi would be glued to my side. When I did homework, he plunked himself really close and scribbled on sheets of paper with his crayons. Leaving him ripped my heart apart, but I didn't know what else to do. I wasn't safe. I told Sita and my mother what those men did to me. Sita didn't care. My mother didn't believe me. No one cared. And if I wasn't safe, what good was I to him? I knew I had to get away. I had to survive if I was eventually going to be able to take care of Navi too.

I lean against the counter and press the photo to my chest, feeling my eyes burn. But then another image comes. Another boy with curly black hair. I close my eyes tightly, trying to see past the rolling fog that splinters his face. Who is this boy? Why can't I remember him?

"Kalli, you okay?"

"Yeah, all good, Ellis."

There is nothing in my bag that's suitable to wear. I pick at my few tops. Perhaps, if I somehow tie them up, I can transform them into something that would catch Ellis's eye. For the first time in my life, I'm actually trying to attract a guy's attention. For the first time, I feel like a normal teenager. After several attempts, I realize that nothing can be done. I am stuck with a choice between a tattered blue T-shirt and a red one. His eyes are blue, so I pick blue. I roll up the sweatpants Ellis loaned me, hoping he won't mind if I sleep in them, and leave the bathroom feeling defeated.

"Perfect timing. I just changed the sheets on the bed. It's all ready for you," he says, beaming.

I wrap my arms around myself, and dig my fingers into my ribs. What was I thinking? I'm not a normal girl. I can never be. Just the mere mention of a bed sends me reeling.

"But what about you?" I ask.

"Me? What about me?"

"Where will you sleep?" I try to keep my voice casual.

"Don't worry about it." His lips curve up at the corners. "As you can see, there are lots of options." He nods at the several brightly colored sofas.

I let my arms fall at my side. "I can sleep on those," I say, trying to keep my voice light. "You shouldn't give up your bed."

"It's not a problem. I want to." His hand brushes against my cheek.

And before I can protest anymore, he scoops me into his arms, and my heart hammers against my chest. But for the first time in a long time, it is not out of fear.

He gently tucks me in. There is so much I want to say to him, somehow, to let him know how grateful I am, but I can't speak.

"Sleep well, Kalli," he says, kissing me lightly on the top of my head.

I close my eyes, knowing I will never fall asleep again. I will just replay the last few moments over and over and over.

EIGHT

Sita has found me. I have no idea how she did it, but she has, and she has brought a fresh recruit with her. He holds me down. I can't break away. Sita's telling him that if he agrees to marry me, he doesn't have to stop. He can go all the way. I can't see anything. It's pitch black. I thrash back and forth, trying to scream. Maybe if my mother actually sees what is happening, she'll do something to stop it. To stop them. She'll have to believe that I wasn't making it all up.

"Mom! Help me! Please!" But my cries remain silent and only a gush of dry air escapes my lips.

I can feel his hot breath on my face. I shake my head as fast as I can, unwilling to let him put his disgusting lips on me. I punch and kick and bare my teeth and snap wildly. I thrash my arms, but he's holding me down even harder, shaking me. He's shouting something.

"Kalli! Wake up, Kalli!"

And then suddenly there's light, a lot of light. I see him. His face is on top of mine, his eyes wide and crazy.

"Kalli, wake up. You're okay," his voice pleads.

I know that voice.

"Ellis?" I ask shakily.

"Yes, it's me. That was some nightmare. You've been

kicking and screaming, and I couldn't wake you."

I look down at my legs wound up in the sheets. I sit up to free myself. "I'm so sorry I woke you. Just a silly dream," I say, trying to still my trembling body.

"It didn't seem like a silly dream."

"I'm fine. Really. I don't want to keep you awake."

"Shhh. It's okay." He adjusts the covers back over me. "Go back to sleep, Kalli. It's still dark outside."

I lie down, close my eyes, and keep still. But it's difficult to shake off the nightmare. I haven't had one that bad in a long time. My legs are uncooperative and continue trembling.

I raise my eyelids to see Ellis get up and adjust the covers so that they are nice and flat again.

He must be annoyed. But instead of walking away, Ellis sits beside me.

"I'll stay with you, if that's okay?"

Is it okay? The last time a man was in bed with me, he …. I shudder at the memory. But Ellis is not like them. He's made no attempt to hurt me. He's only been kind.

He looks at me, waiting for my answer. "You don't have to," I say.

"I know I don't have to. I want to. But only if it'll help," he says.

I take a deep breath and nod. He's different, I remind myself.

He wraps his left arm around me and pulls me in close against him, so that my head rests on his shoulder.

"Now you close your eyes. I'll be right here beside you."

71

I do as he says. The terrifying nightmare and the excitement of being so close to Ellis has me all wired up. The horrible images I saw beneath my closed eyelids insist on replaying. I can't stop them. And then there's Ellis. We're separated by the covers, but I can still feel him. The warmth coming from him settles my shivering legs, though I don't expect to sleep.

But I must have drifted off, because when I wake, I find Ellis beside me with his head flung back over the headboard, asleep. I shut my eyes and clear my mind, so this magical moment can find a permanent place in my memory. He stirs beside me, and I stay still, hoping to stretch this out a while longer. I lie there listening to the house waking up.

"Mmm," he breathes, as he shifts and opens his eyes.

"Good morning," I say, sitting up beside him. "I can't believe you sat here the entire night. It can't have been comfortable."

"No, it was fine." He massages his neck. "How about some breakfast? I know Lucy and Bo are hungry." He gestures to where the cats pace impatiently.

"Yeah, breakfast sounds great."

The next couple of days pass quietly. There aren't any intrusions from Fallon or Margaret. And my doubts about Ellis have finally been put to rest. He has been nothing but kind and attentive. I was right to trust him. The only disturbances are my nightmares.

During my sleep, I go places Ellis can't follow. Places of horror. Places from my past. I'm trapped until Ellis, shaking me and calling my name, pulls me free. Every night I try and stay awake for as long as I can, but inevitably I drift off, nestled in his arms.

I don't understand why the nightmares have begun again. It has been at least a month since I had one. Of course, I wasn't surprised that the nightmares invaded my sleep when I ran away. That first night on my own had been terrifying. It had been uncommonly cold. My blanket wasn't thick enough to keep the chill out, so I sat shivering under a play structure at a park. Too afraid to close my eyes, I huddled in a tight ball and watched the darkness come. Every sound made me jump. But the need for sleep eventually pulled me in, and I went to a place even more frightening.

I was relieved that I had survived the night and that the dream was over, but scared because I didn't know what to do next. I couldn't stay in the park since parents were showing up with their kids to play. So I slunk out and wandered the city, trying to figure out my bearings.

I found myself going in circles most of the day until I came upon the train station. It was crazy busy, so no one took notice of me. There were places to buy food, washrooms, and it was warm. It was better than sleeping outside, but I hope I never have to go back.

I've fallen into a comfortable rhythm living with Ellis, and I don't want to lose the consoling repetition of it. We make delicious meals together, read side by side, and we talk a lot. Even though we've been together for such a short time, I feel like our lives have always been enmeshed.

Now we sit side by side, at the kitchen table. My hands held snugly within Ellis's. All the walls I'd built to hold in my secrets have been crumbling away.

I had told him that I wanted to talk to him about something after dinner. I hadn't meant to be mysterious, but obviously I had. He's trying to be patient, but his eyes betray him. I've started to read his silent gestures and facial expressions. Ellis's eyes blink rapidly, clearly indicative that he's nervous.

I lean my head back, close my eyes, and take a deep breath. I allow the secrets I've hidden so deeply to find their way to the surface.

"I never told you the actual reason I left home." I swallow hard. "It all started pretty much as soon as my dad left. I realized I was on my own. No one was going to help me. But the hardest part of saving myself was—" I choke back a sob. "The hardest part was leaving Navi, my brother. I had no choice."

"Why, Kalli? What happened?"

I've kept this secret locked away for so long. But he's looking at me with his kind eyes, and I feel safe.

"Once my dad left, Sita worried we'd become destitute. She didn't think my dad would honor his promise to financially take care of us. So she decided to marry me off into a rich family."

I pause, feeling myself being pulled into that moment when she proudly shared her plan. I had been appalled, but assured by the certainty that my mother would never allow such an atrocity. I quickly realized that this was not to be the case. My mother rejoiced in the possibility that I would marry into a good Indian family.

"Marry someone? That's ridiculous!"

"In India arranged marriages still happen. Certainly not the deranged way Sita went about it, but they do exist." I cringe at the memory of men so much older, so disgusting, reaching out and touching me.

Lucy jumps up on my lap. I run my fingers through her soft fur and allow her purring to steady my breathing.

"I don't get it, Kalli. How could your mom agree to all of this? How could she let you go so easily?"

I shrug, not knowing the answer to this question. How *could* she let me go so easily?

I don't want to talk about this anymore. I twist the ends of my hair. "Um, I'm getting kind of tired." I stand up, feeling jittery. I cross my arms and dig them into my sides. My legs twitch. I can't still my body.

He regards me carefully, trying to keep up with my sudden change in mood. He doesn't understand. How could he? He thinks I ran away to escape an arranged marriage. I can't change his impression. It's too disgusting to say out loud.

"Yes, of course," Ellis says, getting up. "You get some rest, and I'll pop out for a bit. Run a few errands. Will you be okay here on your own?"

"I'll be fine. I didn't even have a nightmare last night." I try to smile. "So I guess your night duty is finally over, and you can get some real sleep."

"Don't worry about it," he says, squeezing my shoulder.

He leans over and gives me a quick peck on the cheek.

And with that tiny gesture, he makes me believe that happiness can exist, despite what almost every memory I have tells me.

I watch him shut the door as he leaves, and then I get into bed. I hope, somehow, that the last few days with Ellis will wipe away the pain of the past and allow me to fall asleep dreamlessly.

I close my eyes, but sleep evades me. I wait. I shift. I throw covers off and then snatch them back up. Then it dawns on me. It's the first time I've been alone since coming to Ellis's house. I could easily leave if I wanted to, but all I want is to stay here. To stay with him. I know my appointment with Margaret is coming up, but even the prospect of seeing her no longer seems threatening.

The wind smacks against the windows. I listen to the house creaking, as if my presence has made it feel uncomfortable too. Though I've been staying with Ellis for a few days now, the place feels unfamiliar without him. I try to cajole the cats into bed with me, but they're fast asleep in the trees. I get up, not sure what to do with myself. I'd been spared the nightmare last night, but I'm worried that, without Ellis nestled beside me, it'll return with a vengeance.

Maybe a book will help. I make my way to one of the walls lined with books, when I see the phone. It's one of those old dial up phones. It's like the ones I'd seen in *It's a Wonderful Life*, my dad's all-time favorite show. How ironic, that my dad ended up turning his back on his life. I guess he didn't think it was wonderful anymore.

For a split second I think about calling him, but then I picture the last time I saw him. He hadn't called me in a long time, hadn't returned any of my messages, even though I had said I really needed to talk to him. So I'd hopped a bus to go to see him, to tell him face to face what was happening to me. My chest tightens as I relive the moment I walked up to his house and heard the laughter. I saw them through the window. My dad and a woman I had never seen before. Arms wrapped around each other. Kissing. She got up, displaying the huge bump beneath her dress. She was having a baby. He'd made himself a new family and had forgotten all about Navi and me. My dad's betrayal hurt more than my mother's. I always suspected she was weak, but I'd held him up to a higher standard. His fall from grace has left a deeper scar.

The phone trembles in my hand, pulling me from my memory. I will never forget his desertion. I will never call him.

I decide to try Mim. As I bring the receiver to my ear, I hesitate. Talking to Mim is wonderful and painful at the same time. I love the sound of her familiar voice, but it also makes the pangs of sadness stronger when we say goodbye. I shut my eyes and picture Mim with her round baby face and long blonde braids dangling down her back. I envision her black eyes, striking against her pale skin. I place my finger in one of the numbered circles and start dialing.

"Hello?" The sound of her voice is like home to me.

"Hey, Mim, it's me,"

"Kalli? Oh my God! Are you okay?"

"I'm okay. What about you?"

"When are you coming back?" she asks, as if not hearing me.

"I—"

"Where are you now?" she insists.

"I—"

"Why haven't you called me in so long?"

"Well—"

"Where are you?" she asks again.

"Mim, hang on, you're not letting me get in a word."

"Sorry. I've been so worried."

"I'm fine, Mim. Actually better than fine. I met this guy—"

"What!"

"I got into a bit of trouble, and he helped me. He's really nice, and I've been staying with him …."

"WHAT?"

I pull the phone away from my ear. Her shriek even wakes the cats.

"I know. It's crazy, but it's amazing," I say, my cheeks reddening and my stomach fizzing.

"So are you *living* living with him?"

"Oh my God, no. But he's so good looking."

"As good as Bradley?"

It's as if her hand reaches through the phone and tightens around my neck. I can't breathe. How could she mention him?

"You know, he asks about you," she says, as if that's an

excuse to bring him up. "I think he still likes you."

Calling was a mistake. I thought talking to her would make me feel better, like it did all the other times. But hearing Bradley's name only makes me ache all over. I remember him crossing the gym, his eyes glued on mine. I wished I'd danced with him. All the girls liked him. I couldn't believe he even asked me to dance. And then I ran out on him. I wish I'd been a normal girl who could dance with a guy and not freak out. One more thing Sita took away from me.

"Kalli, you still there?"

I think about hanging up, but I can hear the panic in her voice. She knows she crossed a line.

"Yeah, I'm still here."

"I'm sorry. I know I shouldn't bring him up."

"It's okay. I'm over all of that," I lie.

"Are you really okay? You said you got into trouble."

"What?"

"You said that guy helped you when you were in trouble. What happened? Is that little boy with you?"

"What? What did you say?"

"The boy? I think his name was Simon."

My knees buckle and I grip the table for support. No, not Simon. Sammy.

The phone slips from my hand and falls to the floor, just as the door opens and Ellis comes in, bringing a gust of cold air that encircles me.

NINE

Sammy? I can't hear, see, or think clearly. Everything is muted. I know Ellis says something to me because his lips move. His eyes are wide as they move rapidly from the phone dangling off the table to me. He yanks up the cord and then grabs onto my shoulders, shaking me, so that the phone bounces against me.

"Who are you talking to?" he demands.

I am vaguely aware of another sound emanating. But from where? Ellis's lips have stopped moving, but the screeching hasn't.

Sammy? How could I forget? My head throbs as a rush of images circle my brain. And through it all, I can still hear the shrieking. It's coming from the phone. Mim. I place my hand on the phone and try to pull it up to my ear, but Ellis won't let go. His face is hard and angry. I tug until he finally releases the phone. His eyes have narrowed and his lips are pursed tightly. I'm shocked at how closely he resembles Fallon.

"Who is that? Is that him?" Mim bellows into my ear.

"Sorry, Mim. I'll call you later." I hang up, even though I can still hear her frightened voice.

Ellis is standing over me, his face red, but it doesn't matter. Nothing matters except Sammy. I have to go back.

I have to get back to him. He must be terrified. I push my way past Ellis and race for the door. Ellis grabs on to my arm and I jerk it away. He recoils.

"Kalli, who were you talking to?"

There's no time for this. I need to get out of here and back to Sammy. I feel sick. How could I forget about him? How could I have spent these past days living in such luxury while Sammy has been struggling all alone on the streets? I feel myself suffocating under the weight of my shame.

"Kalli!" Ellis's roar shocks me from my thoughts.

"I have to go. He's out there."

"What are you talking about? Who's out there?" Ellis is beside me now, holding onto my arm and anchoring me to the spot. "Who were you talking to?" I'm taken aback by his anger. He's never spoken to me like this before.

"I have to get Sammy!"

"Sammy? Is that who you were talking to?"

"What? No, of course not. I was talking to Mim. And she asked about the little boy and then …." I can barely say it. "I remembered," I choke out. "I remembered Sammy."

Ellis lets out a deep breath and his arms fall to his side. "You remember?" All the rage in his voice has been replaced by fear.

But then the meaning of his words hit me. "You know about Sammy?"

"Kalli, come sit down with me," he says softly.

"No. I can't sit down." I look at him uncomprehendingly. "I have to get to Sammy. I have to get to the train station. I hope he found his way back there."

"You can't," he says.

"What do you mean I can't? Am I a prisoner here?" I run my hands through my hair, causing the skin on my face to pull back.

"Of course you're not a prisoner. But please come sit down. I need to tell you something."

He sounds so ominous. But I can't deal with whatever dilemma he has right now. All that matters is getting back to Sammy.

"Come with me. We'll go in that incredibly fast car of yours. We can talk on the way," I offer, rushing to the door.

My fingers are turning the knob when he pulls my hand away.

"What are you doing?" I demand, turning on him.

"You can't go to Sammy," he whispers.

"Of course I can. Listen, if you don't want to take me, that's fine. But I'm going."

Ellis rests his palm on my cheek. He looks completely miserable. He doesn't want me to go. He wants me to stay here with him. He's falling for me. I place my hand over his.

"I won't leave you. I'll just go and find Sammy. Make sure he's okay." And then the most wonderful thought comes to me. "Maybe I can even bring him back too. He's so little and really wouldn't be any ...."

Ellis is shaking his head. "You can't go to Sammy. He's not at the train station."

My hand falls limp beside me. "What do you mean he's not there?" A slow panic bubbles inside me.

"Please come and sit down," Ellis says, putting his arm around my shoulder, trying to guide me to the sofa.

I duck out from under him. I swallow. My throat is suddenly so dry. "What do you mean he's not there?" I repeat.

Ellis takes a deep breath and bites his lower lip. "When I found you in the alley, you were badly hurt. You were covered in blood. I knew I had to get you help quickly." He pauses and strokes my hair. "You were delirious. Your words were slurred and didn't make any sense. But you did repeat one name over and over."

"Sammy," we say together.

"Yes, Sammy," he smiles wistfully, causing the ripples of panic to grow into waves. "So after I dropped you off at the clinic and made sure you were going to be taken care of, I went back." He closes his eyes and leans his head back against the door.

Bile clogs the back of my throat. Tears spill over onto my cheek, and I wipe them away. It's not true. What I'm thinking is not true. It can't be.

"Where's Sammy?" I ask, my voice thick and strangled.

"He was so small. It took me a while to find him, huddled in a corner of the alley."

This can't be happening.

"I tried desperately to revive him."

No.

"But his wounds were too much."

"No." My voice finally breaks through. "Sammy got away. I saw him. I remember. We were being attacked, and I fought that guy off. I saw Sammy run out of the alley.

I saw him. I saved him!" I bellow, clutching the fabric of Ellis's shirt.

He grasps my hands within his. "Sometimes when the pain of reality is too much, our brains protect us any way they can." He shakes his head. "I'm sure you did everything you could to keep him safe."

"I did keep him safe," I say, unwilling to believe. "And at the clinic, you all said there wasn't a child. I asked you!" I pull myself free of his hold and shove him away.

"Margaret said that even though she had healed you physically, you weren't ready for the truth. That you had buried the truth about what happened, and it would be best to wait until you were stronger to tell you about Sammy," he says, trying to pull me back into him.

I push his hands away and step back from him. "It's not true," I cry. "It can't be true. I didn't make it all up."

"That guy was strong, and he had a knife. You can't blame yourself. It wasn't your fault." Ellis swallows. "I'm so sorry, Kalli. Sammy never made it out of the alley."

I'm drowning. I must be drowning because I can't breathe. My lungs are full. My ears ring and an unbearable weight crushes my chest. The last thing I hear is Ellis saying, "He's gone."

TEN

I float on the surface of waking. Ellis sleeps beside me. Last night, after he gathered me in his arms, we lay quietly on the bed. Neither of us spoke. I wrapped myself into a tiny ball and prayed I could die.

First I abandoned Navi; then I got Sammy killed. Sita was right. I am worthless and pathetic and selfish. Sammy trusted me to take care of him. From the moment I saw him, screaming at the kids twice his size to stop throwing stones at the pigeons, I loved him. And when they turned their raised arms to him, I didn't hesitate. I ran forward and took my place between him and the flying rocks. From that moment on, we became a team, a family.

I still can't believe it's true. Last night, my mind filled with flashes of him. Pink ice cream dribbling down his lips. Playing with the ends of my hair as he nestled into me, keeping each other warm. Sammy crying out in his sleep as his past haunted him. Now that I think of it, it was Sammy's nightmares that caused my own to cease.

The house is silent and the moon splashes shadows across Ellis's face. The bed is soft and warm, so different from the steel benches in the train station where Sammy and I slept. I am pulled from my thoughts, as I realize what woke me in the first place. My belly burns.

I scrunch up my shirt, and look at my stomach in the broken light, but I can't see clearly. I ease out of bed and go to the bathroom. I flick the switch, and squint in the sudden brightness. I stand in front of the long mirror, exposing my stomach. The skin looks okay. No redness, which hopefully means no infection.

"Ouch!" There's more than just a tingling.

I sit on the edge of the tub and gently rub my stomach with the tips of my fingers. I grab the cream that Margaret gave me, generously apply it, and instantly feel relief.

I'm no longer tired. I feel jumpy and restless. I keep seeing Sammy. What did I say to him? Did I at least hold him as he took his final breath?

I creep out of the bathroom, my nerves tingling and my skin covered in gooseflesh. Ellis is still asleep. I don't want to wake him, but I'm too wired to go back to bed. It's getting lighter outside. The clock by the bed reads 6:50 a.m. I walk to the window and look out into the semidarkness. I haven't been outside since entering Ellis's house several days ago. I put on my worn jacket, socks, and shoes, hesitating only a moment before I open the front door. It's cold. I wrap my arms around myself. The air feels fresh and sharp against my uncovered face. It suddenly dawns on me. I'm outside, completely on my own. If I want to, I can leave. I can run away.

I turn to my left and then to my right. It's totally deserted, just black shadows stretching out on all sides. How far will I have to walk to get back to an area I recognize?

I begin to run. The wind cuts across my face, and I see

that I'm almost at the entrance to the forest. Twigs crack under my steps. There's still very little light. It's almost like moving blindfolded. But my body relaxes and my chest opens up while I take in great gulps of fresh morning air.

The pain in my stomach has vanished. I'm well into the woods now, completely surrounded by trees. The leaves have fallen, but there are tall pines covered in dark green needles, shielding me from the blowing wind.

It's so quiet. I weave around trees and fallen branches. I'm not concerned about finding my way back.

A loud scratching startles me. I stop and hold my breath. I can't see anything. Is Ellis looking for me? I call out to him, but there's no reply.

The scratching occurs again. It's coming from farther into the woods. For all I know, there could be wild animals out here. I decide to turn around and make my way back to the house. The forest, which moments before seemed welcoming and safe, now feels foreign and unfriendly. I am disoriented. I stop to take in my surroundings and that's when I hear the crying. It sounds like a cat. Oh no. Did I shut the front door? Could the cats have gotten out? I search the ground for something to defend myself with in case it's a wild animal. I grab a few rocks from the ground and tear off a branch from a tree.

I cautiously head in the direction of the crying. My head turns to every sound I hear. Suddenly I see a building hidden amongst the trees, and about ten feet away from the structure is Lucy, tangled in the weeds and struggling to free herself. I inch my way to her and carefully pull her out of the plants. I scoop her into my arms. She squirms at first but then settles.

The building is old and ugly. Most of the windows are boarded up. Thorny vines grow up the sides, and I shudder at the wasp nests that hang beneath the gutters.

Hoping the nests have been abandoned, I step closer. The few windows that haven't been sealed up are filthy, covered in dirt and dust that makes it impossible to see through. I wade amongst thick brush and weeds until I find the wooden door. It too is concealed by a mountain of weeds. Lucy wriggles as I try to open the door, which remains firmly shut. Why is an old abandoned building locked? And then I remember—Ellis said he kept his inventions in a workshop. This must be it. It looks so run down though.

"Ow!"

Lucy digs her nails through my jacket, and I drop her. The second she hits the ground, she bolts away.

"Dammit, Lucy! Get back here."

She scurries into the brush and vanishes. I turn back to the building. For some reason I'm drawn to the dark and dingy workshop. I'm about to twist the handle one more time when I hear a loud crunch in the distance. It sounds too heavy to be coming from the cat. Feeling stupid at putting myself in another precarious position, I give up my efforts to get inside and focus on finding Lucy and getting back to the house.

Hunching low to the ground, I push aside the bramble, softly calling out her name. The sun is stronger now, so it provides a bit of light in the dense forest, and I finally find her. Every time I inch closer, she runs away. I grab a twig and shake it on the ground so that it scrapes the leaves. Just as I hope, she attacks her "prey," and I scoop her up.

I straighten and realize that I'm completely disoriented. Which way? A wall of massive trees surrounds me.

"Any idea?" I ask Lucy.

I randomly pick a direction and start walking. I'm getting deeper into the dense trees when I startle at the sound of a loud crack, jump up, and whack my head on a branch.

"Ow." My voice catches in the back of my throat. A cold chill fills every pore on my skin. I'm suddenly in a pocket of icy air and my hearing is muffled. I can no longer hear the din of the forest creaking and breathing. Instead indistinct whispers fill the air. My stomach tightens. I have no idea why my response is one of panic. It's probably just some hikers.

Despite the likelihood that the sounds come from someone completely harmless, I can't shake the feeling churning inside my chest. I have to get away from here.

Holding Lucy close, I inch my way as quietly as I can away from the voices. Every leaf or twig I break beneath my feet sounds like thunder. I don't know how, but I find the clearing at the back of Ellis's house.

I run as hard as I can until I reach the safety of the front door and let Lucy down. My fingers almost touch the knob when I feel a weight on my shoulder. I fling myself around, fists raised, ready to defend myself. My hand collides with a chest at the exact instant my brain recognizes Ellis's shocked expression.

ELEVEN

The initial relief that washes over me dissipates. He wears the same cold expression he had last night when he found me on the phone. How can someone look so mean and lovely at the same time?

"Where were you?" he demands.

I level my voice to match his accusatory tone.

"I went for a run. I'm sorry. I didn't mean to hit you. You surprised me."

"A run? Where? Where did you run?"

"What does it matter where?" I ask.

He looks taken aback. "It matters because it's not safe out in the forest."

"What's not safe about it?"

"Hikers have come across bears." He sighs. "Look, I'm sorry. I kind of panicked when I woke up and you were gone."

"You did?" A smile spreads across my face. He was worried. I matter to him.

His fingers gently stroke my forehead, pushing back my hair. "I promised Margaret I would watch over you."

His words are like a slap, and my smile vanishes. I thought we had grown closer. All those nights he held me while I fell asleep. And especially after last night. Had he only done it to accommodate Margaret's wishes? Am I nothing to him?

"It's cold out here. Let's go back inside." He opens the front door.

As he ushers me inside, Lucy darts between our legs and into the house.

"Hey, how did she get out?"

"I may not have closed the door properly when I went for a run. I'm really sorry," I apologize.

"Well, there's another reason not to leave without me."

We pull off our coats. Ellis doesn't help me with mine. All the warmth and familiarity that existed these past few days has vanished. He has altered for me. How can I be so stupid to think for even a second that he would want me? He moves into the kitchen, but I stay rooted by our coats.

"So, Kalli, did you see anything out there?"

His arms are crossed as he leans against the kitchen island. He sounds casual and calm, but his eyes betray him. They are narrow and cold.

"Like what? A bear?"

He stares at me, waiting.

The frosty expression clinging to his face unhinges me. Something's not right. Our connection has been severed, and I feel like I'm looking at a stranger.

"No, I didn't see anything. Except the cat," I lie, feeling the ripple of panic rise inside me again.

"You're sure? Because you seemed like you were upset when I found you?"

"Yeah, well, you snuck up on me. I think you can

understand why that would upset me," I say, meeting his glare.

He shakes his head and lets his arms fall to his side. "Of course. Of course, I understand. I'm sorry. I should have realized. Especially after what you found out last night." He looks like he's about to come over to me but instead stays where he is. "How are you feeling?" His eyes are soft again.

I don't know how to respond. The kind Ellis has returned. I stand by the front door, uncommitted as to whether I'm coming or going. My hand plays with the sleeve of my coat. Last night was awful. Even now, a part of me still can't believe that Sammy's gone. I can't attach myself to the sorrow because my mind insists on replaying the scene that ends with his escape. Twisting the sleeve between my fingers, I just nod.

"You should still keep up your strength. Isn't that what they say?" He grabs a paper bag from the counter and shakes it. "I brought these last night as a treat for breakfast. But ...." He pauses and wrinkles up his nose. "Well, you know," he says simply.

I let the sleeve fall from my hand and take a couple of steps toward him.

"What did you get?"

"The best croissants in the entire world."

"Sounds delicious," I say, my voice distant and hollow. "I'll just wash up a bit."

"Yes. Absolutely." His expression mirrors my own discomfort.

I shut the bathroom door behind me just in time. I grip the counter to steady myself as my whole body begins to shake. I regard myself in the mirror warily. What are you doing? Why aren't you telling him? You can trust him. You can.

"Everything okay in there?" Ellis asks.

"Yup. Be out in a second."

Get it together. The whispers were probably just hikers. Ellis even said that hikers go into the forest.

But the locked building? I'm so paranoid. There's nothing weird about that either. It must be his workshop. He said he kept his inventions in a workshop.

I splash water on my face to smother my irrational worries. I rub each leg to suppress the shaking, dry my face on a towel, smooth out the straggly pieces of hair, and leave the bathroom.

Ellis is standing so close to the door that he has to take a step back as I come out.

"I'm sorry," he says. "I didn't mean to scare you. I just freaked a bit when I got up and you were gone."

"I can't go out? I can't leave? I'm a prisoner?"

"It's dark out. Remember what happened the last time you were in the dark on your own. I don't want you to get hurt."

"Right, because you don't want to disappoint Margaret."

He lifts my chin and stares into my eyes. "No, it has nothing to do with Margaret. It never did. You matter to me. I don't want you to leave."

And then Ellis kisses me. He places his lips onto mine

and kisses me, and I don't pull away. I don't want to pull away. His lips are soft and strong at the same time. He wraps one arm around my waist and, with the other arm, pulls my head closer. My whole body responds and sinks into him. And then as quickly as it began, the kiss ends. I open my eyes to find him staring at me.

"I wasn't leaving you. I would never just leave," I say, meaning it. "I needed to clear my head. I'm having a hard time believing that Sammy is gone."

"I know. It may take awhile for the real memory to come back." He tilts his head slightly. "You could've woken me. I'd have come with you."

"I didn't want to wake you. I thought the fresh air would help. Plus, I haven't been outside in a long time."

"How about tomorrow we go on a hike?"

"Yes, I would like that," I say.

Ellis rests his palm against my cheek. I close my eyes and relax my head into his hand. And then Ellis presses his lips to my cheek.

"Shall we have breakfast?" He leads me to the kitchen.

I close my fingers around his, feeling them intertwine with mine. He looks at me, and once again I'm halted by his astounding beauty. As I watch him assemble our breakfast I realize that my feelings for Ellis are changing. He's more than just someone who provides a safe refuge. He's someone I'm falling in love with.

TWELVE

I lie in bed, unwilling to open my eyes. I want to remember this moment forever. Today is my one week anniversary of knowing Ellis. And after today, Margaret, Fallon, and all things that infiltrate my world of bliss will disappear.

The past couple of days dissolved all my misgivings about Ellis. Being with him is as simple as breathing. I feel safe and warm and, perhaps, even loved.

Neither of us has actually said the three little words, but that doesn't mean the feelings don't exist. The way we look at each other. The way I feel when I fold myself into him. Those moments say "I love you" more than any words can.

It's as if I've known Ellis forever. We grow closer with every second that passes.

With my eyes still shut, I turn to snuggle into Ellis, and my entire body seizes in excruciating pain. It hurts so much that it takes me a few seconds to realize that Ellis is not even in bed. My legs and arms squeeze into my chest, as I try and breathe through the agony.

"Ellis," I groan.

Slowly the spasm eases, and I unfurl my limbs.

"Ellis," I say again, but louder.

The curtains are still drawn, but the morning is so bright that the sunlight penetrates the fabric and speckles the floor. I go to the bathroom and reach for the cream. This simple movement sends stabs of pain exploding in my abdomen. I steady myself against the counter and dab cream on my stomach. The relief is instantaneous, and I whisper a prayer of thanks to Margaret. I look up into the mirror and see a white piece of paper with Ellis's meticulous tiny printing.

Our first snowfall. Thought we'd go on a walk and then have a hot chocolate. Just gone to buy some. Be back soon.

Ellis.

Snow? I hurry to the window, no longer feeling any pain, and pull back the curtain. It's lovely. Soft, fluffy white flakes cover the ground in a blanket. I brush my teeth, wash up, and dab some more cream onto my stomach just to be safe. I layer myself in the warmest clothes I have, and go outside.

Ellis generously replaced my raggedy old coat with a new one. It's a lovely pale green jacket that rests snugly against my hips.

I bend down, scoop up handfuls of snow, and throw them into the air. For a second, I almost lie down to make a snow angel. But then I remember the workshop. There is something about that building that keeps drawing my mind back to it. It was so decrepit. How can he work in that? Maybe I can clean it up, do something nice for Ellis in return for all he has done for me. I breeze back into the house, grab paper towels, some cleaner, and my old library card from my backpack, and head into the forest.

My library card is the only piece of identification I took with me when I left home. A source of comfort, it reminds me of the hours I spent at the library, cross-legged in an aisle with a book. But Sammy showed me its more practical purpose—breaking into locked buildings.

As I wind my way through the forest, I remember that I don't know exactly where the workshop is. I keep having to backtrack. I also am acutely aware of the slow panic brewing inside me.

To calm myself, I imagine Ellis beside me now, his hand in mine, as we walk through the trees. But when I hear what sounds like faint clicking noises growing louder, even fantasizing about Ellis doesn't stop my muscles from tightening. I stand still and look around, waiting for something or someone to come charging toward me, but all I see are two squirrels chasing each other up and down the trees. I shake out my arms and trudge on.

After what seems like an eternity, I find the workshop. It looks dark and worn against the white of falling snow. This will be my gift to Ellis. I'll transform this drab building into something amazing. I slide the card into the crack, unlock the door, and step inside.

It's immaculate. The white cement floor is gleaming and spotless. At the far end is a large steel desk, flanked on either side by filing cabinets that almost touch the ceiling.

There's a corkboard on the wall by the desk with pictures tacked to it. Pictures of girls, of women, and ... me!

The paper towels and cleaner fall to the floor. Folders are stacked at one side of the desk. Fingers trembling, I grab one. On the front is a photograph of a young woman. It's labeled "Specimen 223." I rifle through some more folders. There are more pictures of women, and then I find my folder.

Specimen 271. I lose the edges of myself. I feel like a part of me has disappeared. There are pictures of me walking down streets of the city, in the train station, under a bridge, and in a park. A photo of Sammy and me. I find notes about my parents, Navi, my school, Mim. Notes about my life. I don't understand. Who could know all of this? The only person I've told all of this to is ....

No! It's not Ellis. Ellis would never .... It can't be. There must be some other explanation. I have to get back to him. To show him this horrible place. He'll be furious when he finds out someone is tracking me, following me. Listening to our private conversations. Ellis will keep me safe.

I stumble out of the building and immediately wish I had stayed inside. Streaks of red hair blaze against the white falling snow. My arms flop against my quivering legs. Fallon is inches away, his eyes wide, staring at me.

I fling myself back inside and throw my whole shaking mass against the door to close it. The pictures, the stories, these are Fallon's. He's been following me, stalking me. I have to get out of here.

I frantically search for a place to hide or something

heavy to block the door, but it's too late. Fallon steps inside. I stand frozen, my body cemented in place with fear.

"What are you doing out here, Kalli?"

I stare at him, unable to do anything else.

"What are you doing, Kalli?" Fallon says.

"Nothing. I was just going for a walk."

He studies me and then looks around the room. He strides over to the desk and turns back to me.

"Been snooping where you shouldn't have been?" he accuses.

"What are you talking about?" I say, trying to speak through the thickness that's clogging my words.

"Didn't your parents teach you not to touch things that don't belong to you?"

It's hard to breathe. Fallon killed these women, and now he's going to kill me. None of it makes any sense though. I just met Fallon a week ago. How did he get all those pictures of me? How does he know about my past?

It can't be true. What I'm thinking can't be true. I refuse to believe that Ellis has anything to do with this. Ellis loves me.

My life is finally worth something again, and I'm going to fight for it. And if my efforts prolong my life for only a few more seconds, then so be it. But I will not give Fallon my last breath. He'll have to take it from me.

He's farther from the door than I am. I launch myself through the open doorway. Tuning out the urge to look back, I rush toward a tree, grab a fallen branch, and savagely swing it in the air.

"So that's how you want to play, is it?"

He barrels toward me, and I brace myself, and then he's gone. I spin around. I can't see him anywhere, and then he's right behind me, his breath on my neck. I wheel around screaming and swing the branch again. The branch splinters against his massive hand.

I turn and run, arms outstretched, frantically grabbing for twigs. The trees have aligned themselves with Fallon and are unwilling to give up even one branch. My foot catches on a root, and I plunge to the ground. Fallon grabs onto my legs. I claw at the earth, clinging to the bits of grass and weeds poking through the snow as he drags me toward him.

I try to twist around and kick my way free. I can't believe it's happening again. Just like in the alley. But Fallon is even stronger.

"I told Ellis he couldn't trust you," Fallon says. "I told Margaret she couldn't trust Ellis. I should have been the one watching you. But they didn't listen. And now what are we going to do? Now it's going to be messy and complicated."

"Ellis would never hurt me. Wait till he finds out that you've been following me, taking pictures of me and all those other women."

Fallon stops. He lets go of my ankles, and I pull them back in, wrapping my arms around my knees, shielding my body from him. Fallon crouches beside me, his face inches from mine.

"Oh, really? Has that brother of mine been filling you

with promises of love and ever after?"

"Brother?" I am stunned.

"You mean in all your conversations, Ellis failed to mention his family?"

"You're not his brother. You're lying. His family lives out west."

Fallon howls with laughter. "Yes, I suppose 'out west' is fairly accurate."

Bile rises in my throat. I scream, clenching my stomach. This time the pain is more intense than ever.

"Shut up!" he yells, yanking me upright and dragging me behind him.

I'm surprised my body is still intact. Something surely has taken hold of my insides and is slicing them into pieces. My eyes blur. I bend over in agony.

"Hurry up—shit!" Fallon stops moving. He stares at the ground, his eyes wide, his mouth gaping. I look down too. There on the trampled white snow is a trail of blood.

THIRTEEN

Fallon lets go of my arm, and I slump to the ground. It's wet between my legs, like a heavy period. He lifts me up into his arms and runs. I feel like I'm going to be sick. And then I do vomit, all over Fallon. He doesn't even flinch. Still holding me tight against his chest, he opens the front door of Ellis's house and lays me on the bed. I curl into a tight ball, sweat streaming down my face, my back, everywhere. The pain is unbearable.

Holding his phone in one hand, he removes my coat with the other. Every time he touches me or moves me even slightly, it feels like hands are reaching inside me and ripping me apart.

Fallon shouts into his phone. "She's bleeding. Badly. Yes, a lot of pain. Okay. Just hurry up."

"Stop touching me. What did you do to me?" I push him away.

"I didn't do anything to you. You need to calm down."

"You grabbed me. You cut me."

"Listen, Kalli. I know it hurts." His voice softens. "I know you're scared. But I didn't cut you. I'm not going to hurt you. You're bleeding, and I'm going to try and make it stop."

"You killed all those women. I know you did," I moan.

"You need to be quiet. I didn't kill anyone." He ransacks the kitchen, yanking cupboards open in a frenzy.

"What the hell?" Ellis is back. "Fallon, what are you doing? Kalli? What's wrong?"

"Back off, Ellis. She's bleeding. I need to stop the— Dammit! Don't you have any supplies?"

"Bleeding? What did you do to her?"

"He cut me," I yell. "He has pictures of me. He's been following me. Ellis, help me!"

Ellis charges at Fallon. Fallon grabs Ellis around the neck and shoves him against the island.

"She's bleeding, you idiot. You know what that could mean. Now where the hell is the demerodine?" says Fallon.

I look at Ellis. His face is ashen as he slumps down to the floor, his hands resting on the top of his head.

"Get up and help me, Ellis. I need towels, blankets, something to stop the bleeding. Now, Ellis! Do you want her to live?"

My vision drifts in and out. I see shadows fly across the room. I hear bursts of anguished voices yelling things like, "Here it is," "Hurry up," "too late," and "so much blood." And a voice saturated in sorrow crying out, "Save the baby!" is the last thing I hear.

"Kaaa-leee, Kaaa-leeee."

I hover underwater, just below the surface, and through the ripple of waves I see a vaguely familiar face.

I reach out and touch it, but the face becomes distorted and frightening. The water feels warm and welcoming, so I sink deeper, and as I do, the face above me convulses and moves closer to me. I submerge myself to escape, but suddenly I'm pulled to the surface, choking and spluttering.

"Kalli. Wake up. Kalli."

Someone's calling my name. Hands are gently shaking me, but I can't open my eyes. It's as if they have decided to remain shut.

"Kalli, please." The voice is full of sadness. I know that voice, and I don't want him to be sad.

"Ellis," I whisper, as I unlock my eyes. I'm lying on Ellis's bed.

He strokes my forehead, the feel of his soft hands soothing against my skin.

"Ellis," I say again.

"Yes, sweetheart, it's me. I'm right here."

Sweetheart. I like it when he calls me sweetheart.

"She'll be here soon. Do what you're going to do and do it fast."

The instant I hear Fallon's voice, my body trembles. Then I remember the reason for the rising terror inside me. "Ellis," I say, my lips barely moving. "We have to get out of here. We have to go, right now!"

"We will, but I need to explain some things to you first." He's speaking unbearably slowly. I shake my head. "No. Must leave now," I hiss, as I try to get out of bed.

My body feels bruised. But we have to get out of here.

"Hurry up, Ellis. Margaret won't take long to get here."

Fallon's talking with Ellis as if they're carrying out some preconceived plan, but that couldn't be, unless .... Ellis looks at me with unconditional despair.

"Not you," I say, as grief takes over my soul. "Your brother? Specimen?"

"Please let me explain." He looks pale and tired

I can't speak. I don't want to hear his explanation.

I'm nauseated from the pain, from the humiliation, and from the realization that I have just lost everything. Again. And this time, there is nothing left inside me.

Ellis takes a deep breath. "What you saw in the building, the pictures, the articles. They were all part of a long and complicated research project. I was assigned to you. I was supposed to keep you around, until ...." He pauses, rubbing his temples. He and Fallon exchange glances and Fallon nods. "Until you served your purpose."

I was wrong, there must be something left inside me, because his words fill me with a burning ache, as the first of my tears roll down my cheeks. I don't want to hear anymore. Even after all the crap and torture I had endured at home, there was still a part of me that believed I'd find a way to make my life better. But now I know I never will. I'm done trying. I bury myself under the covers.

Ellis pulls the blankets away, and I see that his eyes are swimming too.

"But it all went wrong from the beginning," he continues. "You were hurt and that made the whole outcome questionable. It's why you had to stay here, and then I got to know you. You now matter to me because of you, not because of the project. I'm not sure how it happened, but I think … I think … I love you." His voice breaks.

My head throbs.

"You think you love me? How dare you!" My hands clench around the covers. "I trusted you, bared my soul to you. And, for you, it was all a game."

"I'm sorry. But I need to tell …."

"I was assigned to you! I served my purpose. Exactly what purpose?" I demand.

Ellis takes my hand. I pull away, and the movement sends a surge of pain shooting through me.

"Just tell her everything. Do it, Ellis." Fallon sounds deflated. The anger that always seemed to consume him is gone. His whole body sags.

Ellis runs his hands through his hair. His lovely, evil hair.

"Kalli, this is going to be hard, maybe impossible to believe, but it is the truth and I can prove it to you. I'm not from your world. I'm what you would call an alien."

FOURTEEN

Everything falls away. The room, the house, the trees, everything.

"I know it sounds ridiculous. But I'm not from Earth. I'm from Istriya. It's a planet very far away."

Fits of laughter rake over my body, bringing with it, fits of pain. He's crazy. It's perfect. I've fallen absurdly in love with a raving, lying, stalking lunatic. An alien?

"Okay, watch this," he says, and then he's gone and reappears instantly beside Fallon, who stands by the front door.

And then Ellis is gone again, this time appearing in the kitchen and then outside the window and then at my side, all before I have taken another breath. How can anyone move like that? It must been an illusion, a trick.

"I know it's a lot to believe, but do you remember the night I found you? You said something to me about flying. Something like 'anywhere is fast when you can fly.' Well, I can't fly, but I can move very quickly compared to you. Everyone on my planet can. Kalli, it wasn't supposed to be this way. But here we are."

I don't want to listen. I won't allow his words to penetrate deep enough to understand.

"What I am about to tell you will seem unbelievable.

But if you are to live, and you have to live, then you must believe."

I don't want to believe. He betrayed me.

"Please, Kalli. Listen to me." His voice is full of warning. And despite my intention not to listen, I can't help myself. And his story winds its way into my brain.

A planet, similar to Earth, located in another galaxy. The people, facing extinction since their females can no longer bear children. Even Margaret, the most renowned healer in Istriya, not being able to help. So they came here, to find women who could incubate their embryos. In three days, their ship will return to take the embryos back home. The memories of all the women they used were to be erased. But according to Ellis, everything has changed.

I need to get away from here. I am a fool. Ellis is not my angel. He's a monster.

Unwilling to yield to the shooting spasms, I throw the covers off and burst from the bed. Ellis stops me just as my feet touch the ground.

"Let go of me!" I scream.

"I can't let you go. Not just yet. Not until you know everything. Listen, I'm sorry, but Margaret's going to be here very soon. There isn't much time, and there's so much to tell you."

I look into his eyes, and for the first time I see him, see him for who he actually is. My fists tighten, and all the fury I have buried inside me comes rushing out.

"You son of a bitch! You lied to me. You knew my secrets. You knew what I needed to hear. You never cared about me. You just used me."

With each blow I send reeling into him, I can see Sita's cold eyes boring into me, I can see my mother's useless eyes allowing unspeakable harm to come to me, I can see my father's vacant eyes as he walks away from me, and I can see Ellis's eyes, betraying me with each false word of kindness he ever spoke.

I ache all over, as if each time I strike Ellis, I've hit myself.

Ellis doesn't move. He remains fixed like a wall. "Kalli, Margaret's coming. When you were bleeding, Fallon called her. He didn't know what else to do."

We both turn to see Fallon, pacing by the front door. "Hurry up, Ellis," he says.

Ellis takes hold of my wrists and holds me so that I'm rooted right in front of him. "Margaret can't know that you remember Sammy. At the clinic, when you asked about a little boy, it was shocking. No one expected you to have any recollection of him at all. When she repaired your injuries, she also injected you with a serum that removed the memory of Sammy. Your bond with Sammy was the only memory we had to erase, so that you wouldn't have any reason to leave. It was critical that you remained with me for seven days.

"Fortunately, you seemed convinced that there was no child, and Margaret was appeased. If she discovers that you now remember Sammy, she'll realize that the memory modifier doesn't work, and she'll kill you and all the other women."

I'm unable to think, to process all he says to me, though I do understand the last part. I won't be a victim again. I turn to run, but Ellis scoops me up easily and holds me close to him.

He whispers, "I do love you, Kalli. I always will," when the front door explodes into shards of flying metal. Fallon screams and falls to the ground, his body shimmering in silver. I watch, transfixed, as Margaret steps over the bits of steel, her face full of rage.

FIFTEEN

Ellis's fingers dig into my sides as his body tenses. "Oh God. Fallon," he says.

Fallon groans. Specks of blood collect where the shards of steel pierced his body.

"I heard there was a problem," Margaret says, nodding toward me.

"What did you do, Margaret?" Ellis says.

"What did I do?" she challenges. "I think we know perfectly well what is going on here."

"You can't just leave him like that."

"I don't see you rushing to his aid," rebukes Margaret.

Ellis's face is sallow. His eyes are glued to Margaret, unwavering.

"Ellis, put Kalli down and come over here and tend to your brother," Margaret says, a note of warning in her voice. "Ellis!" Margaret repeats.

But he doesn't move. "I'll put her down if you give me your word that no harm will come to her. That you will leave her alone. We'll modify her memory as planned. She won't remember any of this."

"Oh, I will make sure she never remembers any of this," Margaret says.

"That's not what I mean, Margaret. No one is supposed to get hurt. That is the most important decree," says Ellis.

"The most important decree is to save our people!" Her voice reverberates between my ribs.

"That's not true. You only got permission to carry out this project because you swore that none of the specimens would be harmed."

I flinch at the word 'specimen.'

"You didn't even come and help us when she was bleeding. Margaret, she almost died," Ellis says.

"We have enough specimens. She was a spare. I didn't expect anything from her, given the state she was in when you brought her to me."

"A spare! Does Fallon know she was a spare? Because he did everything in his power to save her. To save the ...." Ellis presses me into his body with such force that I can't breathe.

"Enough! Those hosts mean nothing. Their only purpose is to help save our people. The Council Leaders entrusted us with this job. We must carry it out," Margaret says.

Ellis sighs and loosens his hold on me. His voice is even again. "We will carry it out, but no one has to get hurt."

"The discussion is over. Do as I say, Ellis, or you will suffer the same fate as Kalli and anyone else who gets in the way," threatens Margaret.

Ellis looks from me to Margaret and with the slightest nod of his head, I know. He has made his choice, and it's not me. It never was. I'm going to die, alone and unloved. He said he loved me, and I almost believed him in spite of everything. I needed to believe him. I needed to believe in the possibility that I could still be loved. But it's not true, and it never will be true.

Tears stream down my cheeks as he places me on the bed. He brings his lips to my ears, but instead of whispering more meaningless lies about his love for me, he says, "Don't move," and then he's gone.

Thunderous sounds envelope the house. Margaret and Ellis become blurred objects moving at such great speeds, that it is impossible to distinguish who is who.

"Enough!" Margaret's shrill voice brings the chaos to an end.

Ellis is at the foot of the bed holding what looks like a large silver candlestick.

"No, Ellis. Don't do it!"

All three of us turn toward the sound. It's Fallon. He staggers toward Ellis, pulling out bits of steel lodged in his skin.

"Fallon, you're okay," Ellis says, relief coloring his face.

"Don't do it," Fallon gasps.

"She leaves me no choice. I can't let her kill Kalli."

"No one has to die. Margaret, we just have to inject Kalli with the amnibitor serum and she won't remember anything. And then the three of us can leave. We have collected enough embryos. We have succeeded," says Fallon.

"It is not that simple," Margaret says.

"Yes, it is," Fallon insists.

"You both have broken the rules of this assignment, and there are consequences to your betrayal. Lessons must be learned," Margaret says, puffing herself out. "This is over. Ellis has made his choice. Fallon, take hold of your brother."

But Fallon doesn't move. "Margaret, just give me the bag. I'll administer the memory modifier."

"Not you too, Fallon?" She looks at Ellis. "I thought I had raised at least one of my sons properly. But you're just as weak."

Her sons?

"This mission will not fail because of either of you. The existence of our planet must remain a secret. I will not risk the chance that any of the specimens remember anything." Margaret reaches into her bag and pulls out a large metal needle.

"Stop, Margaret! What are you talking about? The only reason we came here was to save our planet. Who cares if people know about it? It's so far away, they'll never find us," Ellis says.

"You are so naïve. Of course it matters. I've watched these humans. They butcher everything they touch. They destroy other creatures that share this planet with them. They have a need to seek out, take over, and kill. If they found out about us, they wouldn't stop until they annihilated us."

"That's not true. Kalli is human, and she's the kindest soul I have ever met."

"You are weak, Ellis. You disgust me." Margaret takes a step toward us.

"Don't make me do this," Ellis says, brandishing the long silver object.

Margaret's face contorts. Her nostrils flare, her lips curl. "How dare you! How dare you threaten me?"

"I don't want to do this. Just do the right thing. No one

has to get hurt. No one was supposed to get hurt," says Ellis.

"You were supposed to do what I say and nothing else," Margaret shouts.

Fallon walks between Margaret and Ellis. "We have what we came for. We stick to the plan. We modify the women's memories and leave. No one has to get hurt."

"No. It is too risky. I will not leave any loose ends." She looks straight at me.

"You're not a murderer," Ellis says.

She laughs. "What do you think is going to happen to all those specimens? Once we remove the embryos, there will be no need for the hosts."

"What? You promised the Council that no one would be harmed."

"Ellis, do not be so naïve. Our people are depending on us. They will die if we fail. We were handpicked to do this."

"But you said we would just modify the specimen's memories. Killing is wrong. Please, Margaret, don't."

"Modification doesn't always work. But I think you already knew that." She raises her head toward me. "There have been some difficult cases. And we had no choice but to—"

"You've already killed some of them? When the Council finds out, they'll be furious. 'Cause no harm.' That was the main decree." Ellis is shaking.

"But the Council will never find out." Margaret walks toward me, the needle held firmly between her fingers.

Ellis propels the silver candlestick toward Margaret, but Fallon snatches it. Margaret smiles. She has won. Fallon has stepped in to save her and will use the weapon against Ellis while she kills me. Fallon looks at his brother and then twists the candlestick and lunges at Margaret. Her realization comes too late. She crumples in a heap on the floor with the silver object deeply embedded into her chest.

SIXTEEN

No one speaks. No one breathes.

"Oh shit! What have I done? What have I done?" Fallon runs his hands along his scalp with such force that he stretches and distorts his face.

"Oh my God. Margaret's dead? She's dead?" I'm on my feet. I have to get out of here.

"No, she's not dead," says Ellis. "Fallon, how long did you set the immobilizer for?"

No response.

"Fallon!" Ellis repeats.

"I set it for four hours." Fallon backs away from Margaret's body. He looks small and vulnerable. His bulk seems to shrink, devoured by guilt.

"Kalli, you can't leave. It's not safe." Ellis grabs on to my shoulder. "We have four hours until she wakes up."

"I can't believe I did that. This is treachery. If the Council finds out—"

"No, Fallon. What Margaret was going to do was treachery. We had to stop her."

"But we've only got four hours. What can we do in four hours?" Fallon says, his voice on the edge of hysteria.

"Kalli, I know this must seem crazy to you. You were never supposed to know any of it." Ellis presses his head between his hands. "I wish we never did this. I wish I tried to stop it." He looks up. "I convinced myself that what we were doing was justified to save our people. We tricked you and all those other girls and women. We chose the vulnerable, and we violated your bodies."

My hand strokes my stomach. A baby? The thought makes me want to pull myself free from my skin.

"Was there really a baby inside me? I was pregnant?"

My tongue feels thick and heavy as the magnitude of the question clings to it.

"Your body provided the protective encasing for the embryo to absorb the nuveau flureans. Margaret discovered that somehow humans have almost the same genetic construction that we do, and it would only take seven days for the embryos to absorb what they needed to survive. Then they could be implanted into their mothers and carried safely to term. So you weren't really pregnant. To your body, it was more like a virus that would go away in a week."

"I heard Fallon. He said I was going to die!"

"That wasn't supposed to happen either. It was because you had been injured in the alley. We shouldn't have used you. Your body wasn't strong enough because of the damage from the attack." He's talking fast, as if the speed of his words will make me understand.

"But you didn't care. You did it anyway." I shove him away from me. "You … you invaded my body. You put something inside me. Something living and growing inside me!"

"It didn't hurt you. Margaret prepared your body before she inserted the egg inside you. The amount of our nuveau flureans that passed through your circulatory system will pose you no long-term harm. We made sure."

"You made sure? Just like you made sure that no one would be harmed? Just like you made sure that I would never remember any of this?" Each word I spit out at him drips with sarcasm.

His expression changes in a way I've never seen before. Lines transform his once beautiful face. I turn away, refusing to feel any pity.

"I know it was all wrong. I realize that now. And I know I have no right to ask, but I need your help to fix it." His face is pleading.

I feel like a bomb explodes inside me. "You think I would help you?"

"Not me. But I'm hoping you will help me try and save the other imprisoned women and yourself." He reaches out to me but pulls back before we touch. "The Council doesn't know that the memory modifier doesn't work. They don't know that Margaret has killed and will again."

"So tell them."

"It won't be that simple. Margaret and her team will eventually get back to Istriya too. And they will refute everything I say. We need proof. We need you."

My head feels like it's going to burst. It is all too much. Could any of it be true? Aliens? Embryos?

I touch my stomach. The most plausible explanation is that Ellis, Fallon, and Margaret are crazy, and that I somehow attract people who want to hurt me, that my life is marked for misery.

The other option is to believe Ellis. Believe in the absurdity of aliens. It's unfathomable. Yet there's a small part of me that questions why it can't be.

"Ellis, we need to get going. She has to come. It's the only way." The meaning of Fallon's words make all my muscles tense.

"No, Fallon. We're not going to do that. No more forcing people. It has to be up to her."

"It's for her own good. And for her family's."

"What? What are you talking about? Is Navi in danger?" I ask. It feels like my chest is being crushed under a huge weight.

"You weren't supposed to remember any of this. But since your memory can't be erased. Well ...." Fallon pauses and looks directly at me, his unfinished sentence completed in his eyes.

"Margaret doesn't want anyone to know about all of you. She wants me dead, but if she can't find me, she'll go after whomever she thinks I might have told? She'll go to my home. She'll find Navi and ...." I can't allow myself to finish the thought. Alien or not, Margaret is dangerous.

"That's not true. I don't think she'd hurt your family. It would draw too much attention if people suddenly died. People who would be missed. That's why Margaret said we had to use runaways. Women who could disappear unnoticed," says Ellis.

"Can you promise me that she won't hurt Navi?"

"No one can promise you anything. It's all messed up." Fallon stands up and walks over to me. All traces of his momentary lapse into hysteria have gone.

"So I have to let her kill me. It's the only way to keep Navi safe."

"No! I won't let her touch you. I'll die before I let her get near you," Ellis says.

Fallon shakes his head. "Then you'll die too, Ellis. You can't stand against Margaret. There's only one option that can fix all of this." He turns to me. "You must come to Istriya. We go to the Council and tell them everything. They will keep you, your brother, and those women alive. They are the only ones who can stop Margaret."

"I'll do it," I say. I have no choice. Not if there's a chance that Navi could be in danger.

"Are you—"

I don't let Ellis finish. "But I want to say goodbye to my brother."

"No way," says Fallon. "We don't have time for that crap."

"Shut up, Fallon," Ellis says and then turns to me. He is pale and hollow-eyed. "Kalli, I don't think that's possible. The immobilizer that's in Margaret only works for a certain amount of time. Fallon set it to four hours, the maximum. After that time elapses, she'll be awake. She'll inform the team, and they'll come looking for us. We need a head start back to Istriya."

"Can't you just call someone on your planet? Tell them what's happened and that we're coming. That you're bringing me along." I can't believe the words coming from my mouth. Have I actually accepted that aliens exist?

Ellis gasps. "No. They can't know we're bringing you. They'll shoot us down before we even land. The Council made it extremely clear that under no circumstances are we to bring back anyone from Earth."

"Then I don't get it. If that's the rule and you show up with me, they'll be furious. They won't listen to me!"

"I have a plan. There's someone who can help us. I've already contacted her."

"What? When?" Fallon demands. "I should have been the one to speak with her."

"What does it matter? The important thing is that she'll help."

"Fine. Let's just get going," says Fallon. He's standing by an open drawer in the kitchen. He grabs a handful of long silver rods and stuffs them into a bag.

My throat is thick. I know I've made my decision to leave, but to not even get a chance to say goodbye? Despair floods me as the reality of never seeing my baby brother again sets in. If I stay, Navi will be in danger, and if I go, I'll never see him. There's no easy out. Either choice results in an irreparable rip in my heart.

"Please," I say, my voice small. "I'll be quick. I just want to say goodbye."

"No, there's no time," Fallon declares and walks out the door.

Ellis follows him outside. I wait on the bed with Lucy and Bo, who have jumped up. They're both rubbing up against me, calling for my complete attention. Even the rhythmic sounds of their purring doesn't calm me as it has in the past. So much has happened, and so much more is about to. Am I really going to another planet? It's insane.

Ellis is tense and on guard as he walks back inside. "We can take you to see your family. You won't have much time, but at least it will be something."

I can't help myself. The words just slip out. "Thank you," I say, before I can stop myself.

Within minutes, all three of us are outside, bathed in the glare of the sun on the snow. I'm surprised that it's still light out. Was it just this morning that I woke up excited to share my life with Ellis? It seems like a different lifetime. So much has happened. One day I will process all of it, but now I need to focus on the present. I'm going home. Ellis is about to take hold of my hand when I yank my arm away.

"I'm only doing this for my brother," I say.

I look up at him. It's as if his whole body has collapsed on itself. He is completely broken. My heart stirs, but I refuse to give in. I can't believe I let myself love him.

"You feeling up to the trip?" Ellis asks Fallon.

I forgot that he had been hurt. Fallon's so big, he seems indestructible.

"I'm fine," Fallon growls.

"Hey, what should we do with Margaret? Can we just leave her alone?" Ellis asks, nodding toward the house.

"I'll stay behind," Fallon says.

Ellis grabs onto Fallon's arm.

"Fallon, it might seem tempting, but ...."

Fallon snatches his arm free. The brothers lock eyes,

silently glaring at each other. And then Fallon disappears inside.

"I'm sorry, Kalli, but we don't have much time, and it's faster if I run." He holds out his arms.

"What about your car?"

He shakes his head. He can't be serious.

"You can run faster than your car?"

"Yes," he says.

"That's ridiculous."

"I don't have time to argue with you. If you want to see your family, this is the only way."

"Fine," I say, though it's anything but fine.

I wrap my arms around Ellis's neck, taking in his familiar scent, unwilling to give in to it.

Ellis folds me in tightly. The rush of air pulls the skin on my face, stretching it like Play-Doh. The speed is unbelievable. I've never moved so quickly before. Not in a car, not on an amusement park ride. Nothing compares to this. I imagine what it would feel like if I let go of him. I don't think I would survive. Would that keep Navi safe?

Was it only a week earlier that he raced with me in his arms? The world that I thought existed has disappeared, replaced with something much bigger. Could there possibly be life in black open space? Am I actually going to travel to another world? My head throbs.

Suddenly we stop. In front of me is the place I once called home.

SEVENTEEN

It looks identical to the box-shaped two-story homes on either side. Gray stucco exterior, black roof, and a gravel path that leads to the entrance. A black front door sandwiched between two windows. The curtains are drawn. The house looks dead.

My stomach turns to liquid and my heart aches. I take in my home. My bedroom window upstairs on the left. The other window on the second floor is Navi's room.

"Hey, you okay? Do you want me to come with you?"

Ellis is standing beside me on the sidewalk. I shake my head. I need to do this alone.

I plod up the driveway, hearing the familiar crunch of stones beneath my feet. Each step I take is slower than the one before. I can do this. I have to do this. Navi is so close.

My legs shake as I make my way to the front door. I place my trembling fingers on the doorknob and turn, but it's locked. Automatically, I crouch down and reach under the large stone that always hid our spare key. I push the stone away and there's nothing there. I don't understand. My eyes search the ground nearby. No key. Of course, she removed it. Sita wouldn't want to make it easy for me to come back. This isn't my home anymore.

I try the knob one more time. But it won't give. I stand there, with my hand frozen on the knob.

Suddenly, there are fingers on top of mine. Warm hands against my icy ones.

"Here, let me." Ellis fiddles with the handle and gently pushes against the door. It quietly opens.

I pass through the door with the knowledge that this will be the last time. I stand there staring into the familiar room, with smells of curries, onion, and other spices wafting all over and becoming a part of me again.

Everything looks the same. The front foyer littered with shoes. The front hall cupboard stuffed with so many coats that bits of blue and brown fabrics peek through the crack of the door. There are even coats slung over the short rail that separates the foyer from the living room.

The living room lies in stark contrast to the front foyer. Empty beige walls. A plain blue sofa set against the far wall and two stark white armchairs in front of the window. Between the chairs is the small wooden table that holds the phone.

I remember my mother sitting on one of the chairs, clutching the phone to her ear, as she beseeched strangers on the other end to have their ducts cleaned. I remember sitting around the black coffee table playing Snakes and Ladders with my dad. This room that appears so vacant holds an infinite number of memories for me, both good and bad. A lump forms in the back of my throat, and my eyes sting.

I take a deep breath and step into the living room. My

footsteps feel intrusive. I jerk my head up at the sudden sound of voices. I look at the staircase. My room is up there. It was once my refuge, but Sita changed it into a prison, where all those men did.... I have no desire to go up there. I step farther into the room and cringe as the floor creaks. I think about bolting out of the house. But before I can take another step, she appears. My mother, holding my little brother in her arms. My chest tightens.

I stand there, staring at my mother. I wish I could stop time. I would have stopped my life at fourteen, just before Sita came to live with us. I miss being loved.

Navi starts to squirm. He's gotten so much bigger. He has so much hair. His nose is all scrunched up, like he's trying to figure out who I am. I know it's my fault. I left him. As I take in my home, my mother, and Navi, I realize the magnitude of everything I gave up. Of everything Sita took from me.

"Kalyana. Oh my Lord! Kalyana."

My mother rushes toward me, reaching for me with her free arm. The dark green dress she wears swishes around her ankles as she walks.

I remember that dress. She finished sewing it a couple of weeks before I left. It's made of velvet that she bought on sale. Sita complained that it was a cheap fabric, because it shed so much when it was cut.

I suddenly long to feel the softness of the dress against me. I hold out my arms without thinking. My mother touches my face, and I bury my head into her neck. I can smell the familiar scent of her floral perfume mixed with a hint of curry. I forgot how much shorter she is than me. I feel Navi's hands tugging at my hair. He always loved to grab at my hair.

"What did you say? Did you say ...?" And then the rest of Sita's words get lost in her sharply drawn breath.

Hand clutching her chest, she glares at me. Wearing her red sari, fringed with gold thread, she bellows, "What are you doing here?"

I can't move. I can't speak. My mother removes her hand from my face, and I slowly straighten up. I stare at Sita, feeling my cheeks get hot.

"Figured out you couldn't take care of yourself?" she snarls. "I told you she'd come back," Sita says to my mother, hands on her hips.

Navi fusses and pulls away from my mother, so she sets him down. He looks up at me, with his fingers stuck in his mouth. Suddenly his eyes light up, and he flings himself at my legs. "Kalli!"

I reach down and scoop him up, holding him close. I take in the feel of his soft cheeks, the minty smell in his curls. I'm breathing him in, trying to take in as much of my brother as I can, when I feel him yanked away.

"Don't you dare touch him! Who knows what disgusting things you caught."

Sita's pulling Navi off of me, but he won't let go. He seizes my hair and wraps his fingers around it. He pulls so hard, my scalp stings, but I hold onto him tightly, refusing to let her take him from me. We pull on my brother as if he's a rope in a tug of war. But we aren't playing. Finally my mother steps in and gently unwraps Navi from my arms. He wails loudly and stretches out his arms to me.

"Shh, Navi," my mother soothes, as she pulls my brother into her and takes a step toward Sita and away from me.

Navi hollers louder and starts smacking my mother, trying to break free of her.

"Ouch. Stop it!" my mother scolds.

I can't help myself. I step toward him, reaching for him.

Sita pushes my mother and Navi aside and blocks me from moving any farther. Then she turns to my mother. "Just give him to me."

He screams so loudly that my ears ring.

"Is everything okay in here?"

We all turn to see Ellis walking into the living room. He looks completely out of place in the tiny room.

My mother, Sita, and even Navi freeze.

"Kalyana? Who is this?" my mother asks nervously.

Before I can answer, Sita spews out her venom.

"Who do you think he is? One is not enough for this tramp."

I look to my mother, hoping she will say something. Hoping she will stand up for me and tell the old bitch to get the hell out of our house. But she simply stands there, looking confused and useless. A voice does rise to defend me, but it belongs to Ellis.

"You have no right to say something like that about Kalli," he says, crossing over to me and taking hold of my hand, and this time I let him.

"Right? I have every right. She ran out months ago

without a word. Now she comes back, bringing filth into my home."

The anger and betrayal I have bottled inside me for years comes pouring out.

"Your home? This is our home. My dad's, my mom's, Navi's, and mine. You are a visitor. An unwelcome, ungrateful visitor."

"How dare you?" storms Sita.

"Kalyana, stop. Don't speak to Sita that way."

And then, suddenly, all the hatred I directed toward Sita ignites a million times over and rages at my mother.

"Don't speak to her that way? What about the way she speaks to me? What about the way she treats me? Why haven't you ever said anything to her to stop her from being an absolute bitch to me?"

My mother gasps, but I go on, fuelled by her shock.

"Where the hell were you when she was selling me to those disgusting guys?"

"Stop it, Kalyana. You must stop telling lies." My mother's thick accent is even more pronounced as her voice becomes shrill. Her mouth hangs open for a few seconds before she continues, "Sita was trying to find you a nice boy, from a good family."

"A nice boy? Right. All they wanted was to feel every part of my body. And she knew it. Her only condition was that they had to marry me before they could .... What did she call it? Oh right. Before they could earn complete gratification." I cringe at the repulsive thought. "But they were given a test drive, so to speak. And she was fine with it, as long as they came from a family with money. That's all she cared about. She wanted to marry me off to a rich boy so that she could get her greedy hands on their money. She didn't care that they were ripping my clothes off, touching me …." I pull my hand from Ellis as my fingers ball up into tight fists and my legs feel like springs, ready to launch at my mother.

"That's not true. You must stop saying such things," my mother says.

"She's a liar," says Sita. "Just like her father. All those lies he told about sending money. There was no money. So I found you some highly educated boys. It was done for your good, to provide you with a good future." Sita takes a step toward me so that her face is within inches of mine. She is almost as tall as me, but I don't back away.

"My good? When I came to you crying and told you what the first guy had done to me, do you remember what you said?"

"You made up some stupid lie. I knew the family," she yells back, leaning in even closer so that I can taste the mixture of curry and onions on her breath.

I pull back, repulsed by the odor.

"You said that I was a filthy piece of garbage. That I was like my pathetic mother who got pregnant and married white trash. You said that I better shut up and take it. You said you didn't want to live in this lousy shack forever and that the only way out was to marry me into a rich family. And that the guys deserved to know what they were getting. You told me keep my mouth shut and do it."

I walk past Sita toward my mother, who's gripping the cuff of her own sleeve so tightly, her knuckles bulge. But still she remains silent.

"And you. You did nothing to help me. You let her use me."

"No one used you. Stop making up such terrible things." My mother glances sideways at Ellis. He's a stranger and dirty laundry is never to be aired in front of a stranger. "Kalyana, please, you must stop all of this," my mother implores.

"Get out of my house," says Sita. "You are your father's daughter. White filth. You deserve all the misery in your miserable life. You are not worthy of anything more."

I'm about to speak, to lash back, when the meaning of Sita's words sink in. For an instant, it's as if I'm not physically in the room anymore. I'm looking down at a scene playing out. Then the moment passes and, for the first time in my life, I have clarity.

I take my little brother into my arms and kiss the top of his head.

"I love you, Navi."

I whisper to my mother to keep him safe. To be watchful. To be his mother. Without giving Sita another glance, I turn and walk out of my house for what I know will be the last time.

When I reach the sidewalk, Ellis holds his arms out to me, as if he expects me to collapse into them. Yesterday I would have, but today I don't. I stand in front of him, unwilling to be a victim, unwilling to let my past determine my future. I am worthy of love and happiness. And with this newfound resolve, I turn to Ellis and say, "Let's go."

EIGHTEEN

The trip back is incredibly fast. Ellis pushes himself to make up for lost time. Neither of us speaks. For the first time in a long time, my world is actually completely silent. My head is uncluttered. And I am beginning to see things as they truly are. What happened to me wasn't my fault. What my mother allowed to happen to me—it wasn't my fault.

When we return to Ellis's house, Fallon is waiting for us, arms crossed.

"Took your time."

"Shut up, Fallon," Ellis says.

"You're such an idiot. You know how much time we lost while you said your sweet goodbyes!"

"I said shut up."

"So I take it your family reunion was successful?" Fallon says to me. I thrust my hands into my pockets and look away from him.

"Everything okay inside?" Ellis asks.

"Well, those cats have been circling Margaret. You need to do something about them." Fallon nods toward the house.

"What's going to happen to Lucy and Bo? I suppose you'll just abandon them and let them die." My voice rises in a whine.

"Of course not. I found them a good home."

He is a master of his features and capable of great deception. "Really?" I ask skeptically.

"No, he's going to dump them in some river," sneers Fallon.

"You're such a jerk." Ellis glares at Fallon and then turns to me, his eyes instantly soft. "I promise. I found them a really nice home. I knew I wouldn't be here very long. I just took them in because—"

"Because you're an idiot who thinks you can help everyone and everything," Fallon says, his meaning clear as he looks directly at me.

"They will be taken care of," Ellis says.

"But how?" I ask.

"Let's just say I can be persuasive."

"Yeah, that I can believe," I say, feeling the anger return.

Fallon disappears into the house, and Ellis is about to follow him. I tug at his sleeve and he stops. I know we have to get ready to leave. But I need to know. His answers won't dissuade me from going to Istriya. Nothing will. Navi must be safe. But I deserve the truth.

"Did you already know why I ran away when you found me in the alley? Did you know what happened to me?" I try to keep my voice even.

Ellis glances toward the front door but doesn't go inside. "I knew you ran away. That's why you were selected. But I had no idea why you left." He pauses and regards me with such resignation. "I only learned those things from our conversations. I've broken your trust in so many ways."

134

"You only use women who can disappear? Isn't that right?"

He nods.

"Women who aren't cared for. Have no family. No friends."

He nods again, his head hanging.

"So that's why you wanted to know about my family? Wanted to test me to see if I would call them. Even at the clinic you were checking. What would you have done if I wanted to go home?"

He fidgets uncomfortably and looks so miserable that I steel myself.

"All the other women we used were tranquilized for the seven days it takes to incubate the embryos. But with the injuries you sustained in the alley, this was not a feasible option for you."

"So what would you have done?" I ask icily.

He moans slightly. "Locked you up until the process was complete and then modified your memory."

He looks so pained, but I don't care. I need to know more. And his answer to my next question has the potential to shatter my world into a million pieces.

"Did you arrange for that guy in the alley to attack me? Did you kill Sammy?"

His eyes widen as his hands move to his chest. He opens his mouth to speak but all I hear is a gurgle. I press on.

"Was the psycho in the alley one of you? Was he part of the plan to lure me toward you? So that you could rescue me, and I would be grateful and trust you?"

"No," he gasps, as he regains his voice. "Of course not. The attack on you was a complete shock to me. I was planning on meeting you the next morning, so I was keeping track of your whereabouts. The attack is what made your body weak and unable to incubate the embryo." He shakes his head. "No, we did not set up the attack."

"And Sammy?"

He doesn't say anything. I choke back a sob. "You killed him?"

"No. Kalli, Sammy's not dead."

"What? What do you mean? You said you found his body." And then it hits me. "You lied! You made me think he was dead." I pound my fists into his chest. I hadn't thought he could hurt me any more than he already had.

He grabs my hands and holds them still. "I couldn't let you go back. I couldn't let Margaret find out that the memory modifier didn't work. She specifically targeted your connection with Sammy. All your other connections to people didn't matter. You'd already run away from them on your own. But Sammy. If you remembered him, you'd never have stayed with me. And like I said, tranquilizing you wasn't a safe option. So when you remembered him, I panicked. I didn't want her to hurt you. My feelings for you were changing. I was falling in love ...."

I hold up my hand. "Don't you dare! You sicken me. I hate you."

"What the hell is going on?" Fallon's yell startles us, and we jump away from each other. "So all is forgiven?" He sounds disgusted. "Are you two going to die a tragic death, or are we still going?"

"You are a complete jackass," Ellis says to Fallon.

Fallon's eyes blaze red, yet he says nothing. He rushes by us, heading to the forest. Ellis takes my hand. I snap it back and follow Fallon into the woods.

I'm almost within an arm's reach of Fallon when he stops. He turns to me with his finger on his lips, his eyes searching wildly. I hold my breath, desperate not to make a sound. Ellis and Fallon rapidly gesture at each other as I stand still. I can hear the rustling too. It's faint, but it's there, distinct from the whistling of the wind. Someone or something is out there. Fallon runs in the direction of the sound.

Ellis steps toward me. I know what he's about to do. What I have to let him do. He picks me up and we tear through the trees, away from Fallon. After a few moments, he stops by a large pine and lets me go.

"Did you hear? So many voices, like a small army. I don't get how they found out. Fallon, the idiot, thinks he can take them all on." Ellis paces, his rants muted but alarming.

Ellis finally looks at me, his eyes wide and his skin damp with sweat. He takes a couple of deep breaths. "Sorry, Kalli. Listen. It's going to be okay."

"Okay? What are you talking about?"

"I wish I could just let you go. I want to. But it's too late. They're coming. They'll find you. I can't hide you from them. Margaret inserted a tracking device inside you."

Tracking device? I search my body, pulling at my skin. Where?

"Don't worry. Fallon knows how to get it out. He'll be back. It's going to be okay."

I want to believe him. I'm desperate to believe him. But I've come to know his face, and all I can see is fear. The fear that made him run faster than he ever had. The fear that makes him lie to me now. He knows we're both going to die. Ellis picks me up again, and we race on.

It's strange how a living body reacts to the knowledge that it soon will no longer be alive. My heart beats fast, as if trying to accomplish a lifetime of beats, before it's all over. My hands shake, trying to move as much as they can, before it's no longer possible. But my breathing is slow, almost nonexistent. My lungs are the first to accept their fate.

We reach the workshop, and Ellis sets me down. We walk inside. It's like entering my coffin. I'm certain that I will never leave this place again. The door creaks slightly, and Ellis curses under his breath. We both freeze and wait, but nothing happens. Someone has been here. The walls are empty, the filing cabinets gone, and only the desk remains. And sitting on the desk, taking up almost the entire surface, is Fallon.

"They've already been here. Packed it all up," Fallon says, nodding toward the walls.

"Where are they? Did you see them? What happened?" Ellis asks, as he walks along the edges of the room, feeling for pictures that are no longer there.

"You need to calm down." Fallon jumps off the desk and throws a quick glance at me. "I threw them off our tracks. We have a bit of time before they'll be back. So we better get going."

Ellis moves to the desk, opens a drawer, and pushes a button. The wall behind the desk pulls apart, revealing a narrow flight of stairs. Fallon brushes past Ellis and disappears down into the darkness.

Ellis smiles weakly, his eyes pleading for my forgiveness. I swallow the huge lump building in the back of my throat and feel my way down the stairs. I hear Fallon's footsteps echoing ahead of me.

"Hurry up. I don't know how long it will take them to figure it out," Fallon's voice rings out.

I reach the bottom of the stairs and Fallon's waiting, holding a flashlight. He grabs my hand and pulls me after him.

"It'll be quicker if we talk while we move. Once we get to the spaceship there won't be much time." Fallon speaks over my head to Ellis.

"Yeah, okay," Ellis says. "Kalli, I'm sorry for what you're about to see. But they're not in any pain."

Ellis's lips part again, but this time no words come out, just a tiny moan as we all stop in front of a steel door. I'm afraid to exhale. Who's not in any pain?

After all we've been through in these few hours, what could be so terrible on the other side of the door? Fallon sighs, inserts a key into the knob, and turns it.

NINETEEN

As I cross the threshold, the air shimmers with warmth. Lights flood my vision. Despite the heat filling the room, I feel like I'm encased in ice. I turn to Ellis, unable to comprehend what I'm seeing. But he just looks at me with despair, his arms hang limp at his side.

All around me are bodies. Women's bodies standing in skinny glass tanks, their hair drifting like seaweed. From each tank, extends a long tube that attaches to a large container in the center of the room. Some of the women are rigid and some are slumped against the glass. A bell chimes and a scarlet cloud disperses through the tank. The tube expands as something whizzes through it from the tank and into the central container. The body crumbles against the walls. Within a few seconds the entire procedure is repeated for the next one in line.

His words come back to me. *All the other women we used were tranquilized for the seven days it takes to incubate the embryos.*

Fallon's voice jolts me from the horrific scene.

"I'm going to remove your tracker," he says, grabbing my arm.

I yank it away from him, but he easily pulls it back.

140

"Don't be a fool, Kalli. You don't want them to find you."

I can't believe what I'm surrounded by. It's like some scene from a bad movie. The women's faces are pasty, their pupils white and lifeless. Their bodies are hidden beneath a golden gleam of ribbons floating alongside them.

I flinch. My arm's burning. I look down, shocked to see Fallon cutting the inside of my arm, just below my elbow.

"Ow," I moan, pulling my arm away.

"Dammit. Ellis, hold her still," Fallon hisses.

"You don't just cut someone like that," says Ellis.

"Fine. I don't care. She can keep the tracker," he says.

"The tracker has to come out. It'll be quick and then Fallon will put some salve on it so it will heal almost instantly," Ellis says to me.

Fallon's hands move rapidly and precisely as he pulls back my skin. I expect the pain to be agonizing, but the burning sensation doesn't escalate. Even when he sticks his thick fingers into the opening he's made and fishes around, the pain never increases. But my stomach lurches, when I see what he pulls out of my arm.

Fallon holds out a tiny golden ring, from which dangle millions of thin cilia fibers.

"What is that thing?" My words are saturated in disgust.

"It's called verbindi." Ellis says, admiring the tiny creature writhing in Fallon's hand. "It connects us."

"Why was it inside me?"

"It allowed us to track you. We are given our verbindi as infants. It allows families to track their children and keep them safe. But as we grow, we learn to limit access to our verbindi and can choose who we want to be connected with."

"Aren't you going to tell her the other function of her particular verbindi?" Fallon juts out his chin.

My head turns to each of them. Fallon meets my gaze, but Ellis looks away.

"Didn't you think it was odd, after all you've been through, that you'd so easily go off and play house with a perfect stranger? Even one as gorgeous as him." Fallon nods toward Ellis.

"Shut up, Fallon," says Ellis, still averting his eyes from me.

"What's he talking about?" I ask, grabbing Ellis's arm. He opens his mouth, but doesn't answer me. "What's he talking about?" I repeat.

Ellis groans. "You had to stay with me. It was critical." He finally looks up and I know. I know the truth.

Other than Sammy, I hadn't allowed myself to get close to anyone since I ran away. In fact, even before leaving home, I couldn't trust people. Just Mim. Even Bradley, whom I'd known for years—I couldn't handle his touch. But Ellis—I was drawn to him immediately. Other than my freak-out in his car, I've been desperate to trust him.

"What did you do to me?"

Ellis shakes his head. "Margaret added something to the verbindi, to make you trust me. It made you—"

"It made me think I love you!" Everything starts to spin. My legs can't hold me up.

"No. It didn't do that. I know it's a lot to take in. But

142

what we felt for each other…. What I still feel for you is real. You have to believe me."

I look down at the thin cut on my arm. "I don't have to believe anything you say anymore."

Fallon walks toward the center canister, carefully cupping his hands over the slippery substance. He uses his fingers to turn one of the dials on the outside and a small glass compartment slides toward him. He removes the lid and gently places the squirming creature inside. Immediately, the compartment is bathed in a brilliant glare and then disappears back inside the wall of the container.

"Ellis, the process will take another thirty hours. We attached the last specimens six days ago. If we disturb it now, all the embryos will be destroyed." Fallon's walking around, looking at the bodies, a pained expression on his face. "Ellis!"

Ellis turns away from me. "Okay. That gives us enough time. Margaret won't harm any of the women until the process is over. We can get back to Istriya and speak with the Council. We ask them to spare the lives of these women. It's our only hope. We'll take the secondary ship. It'll be easier to operate without a crew."

"Okay, I'll go get it ready. I'll leave that to you," Fallon says, tilting his head toward me. He rushes past the tanks and disappears into a hallway at the back.

I look at the spheres rolling from the glass boxes into the vessel. Waves of nausea crush me and threaten to overflow. I sit on the ground.

Ellis sits down beside me, and I purposefully slide

myself away from him.

"Oh Kalli, it was real. The verbindi can't do that. It can't make people love each other. It just made you trust me a bit. And even that didn't work so well. Remember the car ride? You're a strong person, Kalli. Stronger than anyone I've ever met. I could never make you do or feel anything you didn't want to." He sighs heavily. "I know you hate me right now. But you'll never despise me as much as I despise myself for hurting you this way. For betraying you."

I know what he's going to say next, and I don't want to hear it. I cover my ears, but his words seep in anyway. "I love you," he says.

I look up at him. Unwelcome thoughts rush through me and weaken my resolve. He chose me over Margaret, his own mother. He made sure I got to say goodbye to Navi. He stood up for me against Sita, even when my own mother wouldn't. And all those moments we shared, surely I'd have known if he was faking. I can feel my anger slipping away, but I refuse to let it go. I cling to it, like it's the only thing I have left.

"I'm so sorry," he continues. "Sorry for lying about Sammy. That was inexcusable. I panicked. I didn't want you to get hurt. If you left, they would have come for you. Margaret would have discovered that your memory was back and she would have …." He shakes his head. "I couldn't let anything happen to you." His hand gently brushes the side of my cheek, and despite my conflicting thoughts, I smack him away.

"It's ready. Let's get going." Fallon's returned. "We have

to move quickly. I won't be able to give you a proper lesson on what to expect, but you will be okay."

We head for a long object, like an upright bullet. The majority of the spaceship is made of silver metal, but one section is transparent. Ellis pushes one of the many buttons on the side and the front half pulls away, revealing a bench. On the other side is a panel with switches and levers.

"Hey!" I say. Fallon has a hold on my arm, and this time he's armed with a syringe. "Sticking me with more of that stuff? So I'll do whatever you want?"

"It's not verbindi. It contains some more nuveau flure-ans," says Fallon.

"New what?" I ask.

"It's kind of like the oxygen that flows through your blood and into your heart. Nuveau flureans flow through our bodies and keep us alive. You need it to survive the trip. We'll be traveling through several different star systems in space and going at a great speed. Please, Kalli, you have to."

I slacken my arm. After all they've shown me, after all they've told me, there's no need for them to lie now. He injects the needle into my forearm. A cool sensation spreads down to my fingertips and up to my shoulder. Within seconds, the chill branches to my other limbs and chest. Fallon nods reassuringly, as if he's aware of what's going on inside me. He helps me into the capsule, eases me onto the bench, and then straps me in.

"Don't I need a mask to breathe into?" I ask, remembering all the shows I'd seen of people traveling into space.

"No, that's what the shot was for. You'll be fine," Ellis

says, as he and Fallon place themselves on either side of me.

"Not afraid of closed spaces, are you, Kalli?" Fallon asks.

Before I can answer, the air erupts into a blaze of angry shouts. All three of us look at each other. Fallon leaps out. Ellis reaches over me to try and pull him back.

"Go, Ellis. I'll keep them off for as long as I can."

"No. We go togeth—" The rest of his words cut off as Fallon jumps out and seals the bullet shut.

"Fallon will hold them off. We'll have a head start. The team won't do anything without Margaret, and she'll be incapacitated for another couple of hours."

But Ellis is wrong. Standing in front of us is Margaret.

TWENTY

My screams splinter off the sides of the capsule.

Margaret walks right up to the spaceship. She presses her hands against the transparent panel, as if she's trying to force it open. She turns and nods to someone I can't see. Suddenly, there's a high-pitched sound. I look for the source. It's coming from a speaker in the panel.

"Good, I have got your attention." Margaret's cold voice fills our chamber. "Ellis, aren't you happy to see your mother has made an early recovery?" she says, with her hands on her hips. "Though most, if not all, of the credit must go to your brother, who re-set the bio-knife." She pauses, her eyebrows arched for emphasis. "You look surprised. I guess Fallon failed to tell you that when he came back to the house, he saw his dear mother lying on the ground and regretted what you had all done. He left before I revived. But I am sure he knew that I would be informing the others of what had happened. So here we are, all back together." She holds her arm out and waves for someone to come over. "Fallon, dear, come closer so your brother can see you and thank you."

Fallon's already massive face is grotesquely swollen, and there's a trickle of blood over his right eye. He keeps his eyes to the ground.

"There was a bit of a misunderstanding, between Fallon and the others. But we have gotten that all straightened out. Now, Ellis, you need to come out of there," she says.

Ellis doesn't flinch.

"Come out now, Ellis, and your life will be spared." Margaret's voice echoes loudly around us.

Ellis lifts his hand. Is he going to do what she says? I realize the significance of Margaret's carefully chosen words. Only Ellis's life will be spared.

"Ellis, re-seal the hatch in the roof. This ship is not leaving. Do not be a fool. They will be waiting for you. They will kill you as soon as you land. You cannot escape."

I turn my head toward Ellis. He's staring with eyes as cold and as hard as Margaret's.

"If that is the way you want to play it," she snarls, and turns to someone I can't see. "Bring him here," she commands. Margaret backs away a few steps.

Voices ring out. Fallon's eyes, though hidden within his swollen head, bulge out in complete shock. I lean forward, pressing my face against the glass, trying to see what Fallon sees, and then I do. A cry of inconsolable anguish erupts from my lips. Sammy.

"Sammy," I scream, banging on the window.

His face lifts and our eyes meet.

"Sammy! Let him go! Let him go!" I shout, pulling at my restraint, which refuses to release.

Margaret suspends Sammy from his collar, as he twists and turns to find solid ground. "I had my doubts about this situation from the moment you brought her in. Your insistence that she not be sedated like the rest. I worried that your ... how should I put it?" She takes a deep breath. "That your weakness would make you forget your responsibility to our mission. So when you mentioned the child, I was inspired." She drops Sammy to the ground and pulls him into her, raking her long fingernails down his cheek. "I sent a couple of people from the team to find the child, and he has been under my care."

"Why would you do that?" Ellis asks.

"Insurance, you stupid boy," she says, thrusting Sammy toward us.

My hands automatically reach for him, as his do for me. He's trying to be brave, but I can see the tears running down his cheeks and the tremble of his lower lip.

"Kalli, you have exactly ten seconds to come out of there, or this sweet little boy will be dead."

Sammy's eyes widen. He kicks and flails his arms, desperate to get away.

"Ten," says Margaret.

I wrench at the seatbelt; my fingers bleed as my skin tears along the edges of the restraint.

"Nine."

"Ellis," I plead.

"I'm trying. It's because I opened the hatch. Everything locks up in anticipation for lift off." His hands are frantically racing across the panel, entering in codes, pushing buttons, and turning knobs.

"Eight."

"Kalli," Sammy cries. I look up and see Margaret grazing Sammy's cheek with a long, thin metal needle. The same one she was going to use on me.

"Sammy, it's going to be okay. I'm coming," I choke out. "Get away from him, you bitch!"

"Seven," she says, glaring at me.

"Okay, I've got it," Ellis says as we both break free from our seats.

I'm twisting the handle, but it won't budge.

"*Aaaahh!*" I shout, ramming my shoulder against the solid glass door.

"Six."

Sammy is full on crying now. His small body shakes and shudders against Margaret, who remains unmoved by his despair.

"Margaret, don't do this," Fallon says, as he takes a step toward her.

"Stay down, Fallon," she threatens and nods her head.

And instantly Fallon is slammed to the ground. An enormous man pins Fallon beneath his knees.

"Five."

"Ellis, let me out of here!" I throw myself against the immovable door.

Please don't hurt Sammy. Please. I pray to any God who will listen. My whole body shakes and my head throbs.

"Margaret, please," begs Ellis. "I'll do whatever you want. Don't hurt the boy. He's an innocent child. You can kill me. Take me instead of him."

A wide grin forms on Margaret's face, transforming

her into the most hideous thing I have ever seen. "Four," she says.

"Kalli, I'm scared," whimpers Sammy.

"Oh shhhh," soothes Margaret, while she runs the metal needle under his chin and up the other side of his face. "Three."

"Sammy, look at me," I say, steadying my voice. "You'll be okay. I love you Sammy."

"I love you too," he cries.

"Awww, isn't that so sweet," Margaret coos, and then her hard edge returns. "Two."

Oh my God. No. Please no. Please. But the door won't give. Ellis is now launching himself against it so wildly that the entire capsule shakes. But the door remains firmly shut.

I see Margaret's mouth open to announce the end of Sammy's life. My ears fill with my screams and pleas for her to stop. Ellis's voice echoes my anguished cries. And then there are shouts from the other side of the ship. Fallon roars, as he heaves himself off the ground, propelling his guard up and out of my view. He charges toward Margaret. Her lips freeze in an open circle, about to say the final number, when Fallon slams into her, sending the three of them tumbling out of sight.

"Sammy," I wail, flattening myself against the window.

"Smash your feet into the glass," Ellis yells, as he lifts me up.

Over and over I kick. It's impenetrable. Outside the chaos continues, until one voice silences them all. My stomach drops. It's Margaret's. She appears again in my

151

line of view, still brandishing the needle in one hand and dragging Sammy along with the other.

"One," she hisses, and plunges the needle into Sammy's chest.

He looks up at me, eyes wide. His body tenses and then goes slack. His eyes relax and his mouth opens, but I can't hear what he's saying.

"No," I cry, pounding my fists against the window. "No."

Margaret removes the needle and lets Sammy fall to the ground. For a moment I think perhaps he's just asleep, that she just injected him with a tranquilizer.

But then his pupils slide beneath his eyelids, and blood trickles from his nose and the side of his mouth. I watch in helpless horror as creases form at the base of his nose, and spread out, cutting into his once beautifully smooth face. The lines widen, deforming him, mutilating him. His body swells to such a size that his clothes rip apart, leaving Sammy draped in rags and disfigured. He lies limp and lifeless on the floor. Someone grabs his bloated ankles and drags his body out of my view.

TWENTY-ONE

My chest rips into a million pieces. My heart feels like it's bleeding. Ellis pulls me away from the window and places me on the bench.

"Well, that was unfortunate," Margaret says dryly.

"You absolute bitch!" fumes Ellis. "How could you?"

"Like I said, that was unfortunate, but if you do not want to see it happen again, you better come out of there," Margaret warns. "Fallon will be killed if you do not come out right now."

My mind shifts, unable to process the horror, and recedes so that everything becomes muted and hazy, as if I am simply watching a scene unfold behind a gossamer curtain. There's a lot more shouting than before, yet I feel detached from it all. Nothing matters anymore. I hear Ellis shouting and swearing and thrashing.

I see Margaret holding another needle. She pulls Fallon into view with her other hand.

"Will you watch your own brother die?" She pokes the needle into his cheek. Fallon's screams fill the capsule, yet I remain seated. Nothing matters anymore.

"Come out now, or I will go deeper."

"Ellis, just go!" Fallon moans, his face drenched in sweat.

Through the milky haze I see Ellis push a bright yellow button. The entire world shakes as flames dance all around our space vessel. Margaret and Fallon are blasted back.

Ellis straps us in and pulls down a lever. Everything inside me, my heart, lungs, stomach, all of it, falls to my feet as we shoot up. I feel like my body is passing through an opening that's way too small.

The capsule is thrashing around and the noise is deafening, but I don't care.

"Kalli? Come on, Kalli. I know what just happened was … was …."

I turn to him and see right past him. He doesn't exist. I don't exist. Nothing exists.

"Please, Kalli. I can't fly this by myself."

My eyes fall shut. I am sinking within myself. Soon, I too will be gone and then all will be okay.

"Kalli! Open your eyes."

Ellis's voice drifts in and out.

"Open your eyes!" His voice is louder and closer but still lingers just beyond attention. He's shaking me and screaming. "We have to get to Istriya before they do. Or all of this, all of the deaths, will be for nothing. Is that what you want? Sammy to have died for nothing!"

His words cut into me and transform my sadness into rage.

"How dare you!"

"I'm sorry. We've been through too much, lost too much, to just give up now." He turns to me, his face sad and his spirit deflated. "I need you, Kalli. I can't do this alone. If you want to just stop, then okay, we'll stop." He swallows. "But if you still want to find some salvation in all this mess, then I need your help. You decide." He turns back to look out the window.

And beyond his face, through the window, I see a light growing, revealing a floating sphere. Earth. A mixture of deep purple and blue surrounded by a swirling white mist and bits of shimmery silver.

Tears well up in my eyes. I'll never be coming back here again. I'll never see Navi or Sammy.

"Kalli, we are going to survive this. I'll figure it out, if that's what you want me to do."

I have no words. I feel numb. Sammy is gone. Navi is gone. But then I remember those women. Sammy would have helped those women. He was only six, but he was always doing what he could to help others. I owe it to him to at least try and be a fraction of the courageous person he was.

With an audible sigh I say, "What can I do?"

My body jostles.

"Hmmm?" I groan, my eyes still closed. I feel a weight on my shoulder.

"We're almost there. Sorry, but you need to wake up now. I need some help again."

I groan again and shake myself from sleep. A dreamless sleep. It was more than I could have hoped for.

"What do you need me to do?" I ask. I stretch my arms

and shake out my legs.

"We're almost there." His blue eyes are wide and awake. "But don't worry, I won't let anything happen to you. I've got a plan."

A plan? We're landing soon. I can't believe we made it this far. But now the end is coming. Margaret would have told them we were coming. They'll be waiting. Waiting to kill us.

Ellis's voice is calm and reassuring. Will he be my last vision?

"Kalli, are you listening to me?" Ellis shakes my shoulders. "Do you understand what I just said?"

"Wh-what?" I rub my eyes.

"Hey, don't let go of the lever. I need you to keep steering while I ...."

"What are you doing?"

The words catch in my throat and I barely choke them out. Ellis slices into his arm, a small trickle of blood oozes from the cut.

"Shhh, it's okay. Just keep your hands on the lever, I'm almost done."

I watch as the self-mutilation continues. Ellis digs his right hand into the opening he's made in his left wrist. His hand's covered in what looks like a golden iridescent gel. He grabs a vial from a nearby shelf and scrapes the gel into it. He places the vial into a slender metal canister.

"Kalli, I've got the lever now. You can let go."

I don't move. My fingers are so tightly clenched around the lever that it hurts when Ellis gently pries them off.

"Why did you cut yourself like that? What was that?"

"It was what we removed from you. It's part of the verbindi in me. It's going to help get us rescued when we land. Now this is really important, Kalli. When we land, you need to—"

"When we land, they will kill us. Margaret said they'd be waiting for us."

"We're not going to die. I have a plan."

"Ellis, stop it. There's no way out. They know we're coming."

I look out the window to see a large brownish-gray sphere emerging behind layers of hazy purple mist. We're so close.

"Yes, there is a way out. The ship needs to land without us in it."

I shake my head. What? He wants us to jump?

Ellis continues to speak as his hands fly, pushing and twisting buttons and switches. He doesn't seem to care about keeping his hand on the steering lever anymore. As he pummels one button and then the other, he reveals his plan to me.

"That's crazy. You think I can jump from a plummeting spaceship?"

"It's the only way. They'll think we died," Ellis says.

"They'd be right!"

"You won't die. I'll get us close enough to the ground, and we'll have these." He holds up a square package that looks like it's made of nylon. "Floaters."

"Floaters?"

"They're like parachutes but can be set off closer to the ground. They will allow us to drop undetected."

Despite his reassurances, I know we won't survive this. I spend the final moments of my life staring at the many colors of space floating by. My thoughts drift between Navi, Sammy, Ellis, and even Fallon. Fallon revived Margaret, knowing that would ruin our chances of escape. His allegiance to his mother doesn't surprise me, but his betrayal to us does.

I watch Ellis as he moves about. Maybe my first impression was right after all. He will be the person who takes me to heaven.

"Okay, we're almost there. I'm going to put your floater on. When I pull my cord, you pull yours. Don't do it before. We have to be below a certain height to avoid detection."

He straps me in. It rests against me like my backpack but lighter. Much lighter. There's no way this insignificant thing is going to save me.

"I'm going to start the self-destruct timer. We'll have less than ten seconds to open the door and jump. Hold onto my hands so we won't be separated. But in case we do drift apart, open the vial and pour the contents out, as soon as you land." He hands me a thin metal cylinder.

"Why me? Why don't you do it?"

"I have one too." He taps his jacket pocket. "Open it, and she'll come."

"Who'll come?"

Red lights start flashing and alarms blare. He pushes another button, and we're blasted with a wall of cold air.

My skin stretches like an elastic band. Ellis grabs onto my hand and pulls me from the falling ship. I can't catch my breath. The air around me whips by.

"We'll be down soon," he shouts into my ear. "No matter what happens, as soon as we land, you untangle yourself and get out of there, and then open the vial."

"What?" The wind is too loud.

"Don't worry about me, just get yourself into the woods."

"Woods?"

"Yes, we'll be near a forest."

I can see the outline of objects moving up to us. A large dark mass gets closer. I take in his face. It will be the last thing I see.

We're spinning around so quickly. How much longer? I don't have to wait long for the answer. Ellis pulls on his cord, and I do the same. Instantly, I'm propelled up. I squeeze Ellis's fingers, but it's no good. He slips away.

Something's wrong. Ellis is still falling. His parachute didn't open.

"Ellis." I know my screams are useless. They won't save him. But I keep calling out to him. Even when I see his yellow parachute finally billowing in the wind, I continue crying out his name.

The ground comes up hard and painful. I can't think. I can't move. Everything hurts. But I'm still alive.

"Ellis," I croak.

My eyes are slow to adjust. Everything is blurry.

"Ellis?" I repeat, blinking desperately.

I stand and untangle myself from the parachute, all the

while scanning for Ellis. And then I see his yellow floater, deflated on the ground about 200 feet away. Fists pumping, I run. I run, even though each step ignites another spasm of pain in my bruised body.

I clumsily pull and twist the straps of Ellis's parachute, until he's free. He's lying face up and there's a stain on the ground beside him growing larger. The barren brown plain stretches out all around. Everything's brown, except the red liquid pooling around Ellis.

TWENTY-TWO

"Ellis? Ellis?" I yell. "Please wake up. Please."

I bring my ear close to his lips, praying that I'll hear the sound of his breathing. Nothing. I look at his chest. Is it rising and falling? I lay my hand on it gently, willing it to move. My hand quivers. Is that from me or from him?

"Oh God, Ellis. You promised I'd be okay, so you have to wake up to keep your promise. Ellis!"

I can't remember the first thing about saving someone. Ellis isn't breathing, and blood is pooling on the ground by his neck and shoulders. His body is all contorted. His limbs aren't lying like they should be.

I need to get his heart going. I tilt his head back slightly, pull open his mouth, and blow air into him. I kneel beside him and rapidly compress his chest. I'm merely imitating what I've seen on television hundreds of times. Am I causing him more harm than good? It's not working. Nothing's working. He's just lying there. I pound on his chest with my fists

"Damn you," I choke. "You completely screwed up my life. I trusted you. I fell in love with you. And you? You abandoned me like everybody else. Wake up and help me!"

I have to stop the bleeding. I roll him onto his side

to try and find the source. There's blood clumped in his hair, but the majority's coming from the back of his left shoulder.

I strip off my coat and shirt. I rip my shirt into pieces. I tie one piece around his head and another under his arm and over his shoulder.

I'm shaking. It's freezing here. I put my coat back on, sit up, and clasp my hands around my knees. Every part of me throbs from the impact.

I stare at his body, willing it to move. My thoughts pass through me. I'm unable to hold onto any of them, like I'm a sieve.

I scan my surroundings, hoping to discover something that can help Ellis. But the ground looks dead. I crawl around and gather a few sticks, having no idea what purpose they'll serve, but at least I'm doing something. I fight back the useless tears that are leaking out of the corners of my eyes.

I'm forgetting something. There's something I'm supposed to do, something Ellis said. The words are there, just slightly out of reach.

The ground beneath me buckles.

"Ellis?" I whisper and move closer to him. Is he finally waking up? I shake him gently. "Ellis?"

He doesn't respond. And again the ground moves. I look around. Through the misty layer of fog, I see thick black columns. The forest. And behind me I can see the orange flames and black smoke of our ship. They will have seen the blazing crash site. They'll be coming. Or maybe they're already close, and that's why the ground is trembling. I need to hide us. We're easy prey out in the open.

I look at Ellis, lying there as the red puddle grows around him. Is he already …? No, he's not. He's going to be fine. After all we've been through, I can do this. I grab onto his wrists and drag him toward the forest. Daggers of pain shoot through me. The blood that's coming out of Ellis trails behind him. A direct path for anyone pursuing us.

There's something in it. I reach over and grab it. It's the vial Ellis gave me. This is it! I'm supposed to open the vial and "she will come." With trembling fingers, I wrench the steel canister open and slide out the glass vial. It's glowing. I pour the contents onto the ground, expecting something miraculous to happen. But the tiny golden puddle lies beside me, useless, hissing.

I continue to the forest. The ground starts to rumble and shake again. I hear voices. They're getting closer. They're coming. I grab him under his armpits, hoping this will provide better leverage to move him. It feels like forever, but I finally manage to break through the first set of trees as the voices and the rumbling grow louder.

"Ellis, please wake up. I don't know what to do."

I bend over and press my face against his. His lips twitch. He's still alive.

"Ellis, we've got to get out of here. They're coming. Please open your eyes."

He's whispering. I bend low to his face. "Vvvv, oo tt."

"What? What did you say?"

"Vial, open vial."

"I did. I opened it. But nothing happened."

"She's coming," he breathes and then slumps back to the ground.

"Who's com—?"

I hear a low hissing sound and instantly, I'm covered in darkness. A bag is over my head.

I twist and punch and almost break free. But whoever has me squeezes harder. I'm wrapped so tightly I'm suffocating. I can't see anything. And then I'm lifted, pressed against someone who's moving quickly.

There's something beneath me. I bash at it with my fist and instantly hear the sickening groan. Ellis's groan. He's under me. We're being carried off together. A couple of times my feet bang into something hard, sending shards of pain throughout my body. I twist and shake, ignoring the intense shot of agony each movement fills me with.

"Stop it! You're hurting him," a voice commands.

Hurting him? Ellis? They're concerned about Ellis. I move around again, but not so roughly.

"Do that again, and I'll drop you right on the spot. And they'll come and get you."

The voice sounds like a girl's. Is this the person Ellis said would come and help us? It has to be. I stay still. I wrap my arms around myself, trying at the same time to feel for Ellis. And then everything stops. I'm dropped to the ground.

"Get yourself out of that," she says.

Slowly, I pull my arms free and remove the covering from my face. It's dark. The low ceiling and walls are made of large black rocks. The ground of dirt is soft and damp. A bluish light emanates next to the girl.

She's brought us to a cave. She huddles over Ellis's body, her hands moving so fast I can barely see them. She dabs him with different liquids and ointments she removes from a bag. She wraps his head in a bandage to stop it from bleeding. My blood-soaked shirt lies beside her.

"Come on, Ellis." She turns to me. "Hey, you, how about some help?"

I rush over as quickly as I can. My head is spinning.

"Get over here and hold his arms down," she commands

"Who are you? What are you doing to him?" I kneel down beside Ellis.

"Trying to save his life. What happened to him?"

"We jumped out of the spaceship so that—"

"Jumped? What a bloody idiot! No, you have to hold his arms much tighter. Get behind his head and hold his arms down. He's not going to like this, but he can't move until the nuveaus get into his system. Use your legs if you have to, but don't let him move."

She pulls out a long, thick needle attached to a large vial of indigo-colored liquid.

"Okay, got him?"

I nod, and she rams the needle into Ellis's chest. He convulses.

"Hold him down! It's not in all the way yet." She's straddling him, pinning his legs together between hers. Her upper body is leaning over his chest as she shoves the needle deeper into him.

"Stop it! You're hurting him. That needle's too long, it'll go right through him," I scream.

"Just hold him down. It's the only thing that might save him." She pulls the needle out.

Ellis trembles all over. I throw myself on top of him to keep him still.

"It's fine if he moves now. The needle's out."

"What did you do to him?"

"Probably just saved his life," she says, her eyes appraising me. "So what about you? Are you hurt?" she asks as she returns all her instruments to a small black pouch.

Before I can answer, a low moan escapes Ellis's lips.

"Adalyn?" he whispers.

"Ellis?"

And it's as if I simply disappear. She shoves me out of the way and rests his head in her lap.

"Adalyn?" he repeats.

"You damn fool. Jumping out of spaceships?"

She cradles him, and he touches her face. They cry and hold each other. I press my knees into my chest and watch them. Ellis is alive, but she's the one holding him, not me. I grip my legs tighter as I sit there. In the dim light, I see the look in their eyes as they stare at each other. I know what that look means. It means love. They love each other. Ellis never loved me. He never looked at me like that. He just pretended to care. Said all the things I was desperate to hear. I'm so stupid. Everything inside me hurts even more than when I fell from the sky.

TWENTY-THREE

I sit huddled in a tight ball, unable to tear my eyes away. I'm an intruder, an outsider peering into something private. But I can't move. And if I could, where would I go? It's not like being lost back home and walking around until I recognize a street or something. I'm on a different planet, stuck in a cave with the man I thought was my angel, but actually turned out to be an alien who came to Earth to ….

Maybe I've gone crazy and none of this is actually happening. I close my eyes and wrap my arms around my body.

"What's wrong with you?" asks Adalyn, with an expression of disgust.

"Nothing," I lie.

"Kalli? Hey, Kalli, you did it. You saved us. I was supposed to save you, but you saved me instead."

Ellis staggers toward me. She's right by his side, holding on to him, her fingers entangled with his.

"Not so fast, Ellis. You should rest a bit more. That was an insane fall you had."

"Not much worse than we have had before. Remember?"

The inside of my chest shrivels up and burns.

"I'm fine. You fixed me all up, just like you always do."

He kisses Adalyn's cheek.

I can't be here. I know I shouldn't care. I told him I hated him, and I meant it. Everything he's ever said has been a lie. He lied about Sammy. But seeing them together—it hurts. I slowly rise to my legs, take a shaky step toward the opening of the cave, and everything shifts. I steady myself against the rocky wall, and I'm almost outside when I'm yanked back.

"What do you think you're doing?" Her voice is cold, much different than the voice she uses for Ellis.

"Adalyn, take it easy. She fell too. Have you examined her?"

"No. I was much too busy trying to put you back together."

"Kalli, are you hurt anywhere? Your head? Back?"

The same hands that touched her now touch me. I shrink away.

"Did that hurt? Adalyn, come take a look. It could be her head or neck."

And then her hands are on me. Poking and feeling along my head. I shove her hands away.

"Okay then." Adalyn moves away. "She looks fine to me."

"It's okay Kalli. She won't hurt you. She's not like Margaret."

At the sound of Margaret's name, my breath catches inside my throat.

"Ellis, we don't have time for this. They could be here any minute. I cleaned up your trail of blood as well as I could, but I was really rushing. We need to move," says Adalyn.

"Kalli, she's right. We have to go."

"Then go. I'm not stopping you and your girlfriend."

"Girlfriend?" Ellis says.

"Are you kidding me? Ellis, we can't do this right now," Adalyn says, tying her hair into a tight ponytail.

"Come on, Kalli." Ellis holds his hand out to me. "Adalyn's on our side."

I don't want to go anywhere with them. But what other options do I have? So, when Ellis calls to me from the opening of the cave, I follow.

A breeze whistles through the bare branches. It's so cold. I wrap my arms around myself. The whole place is gray and ravaged. There's no color except for the ribbons of red and blue cascading through Adalyn's hair. She moves her head side to side, and her thick ponytail sways. The word 'beautiful' is at the tip of my tongue, then she turns to me, and the word dissolves as I take in her face.

She makes no effort to conceal her malice toward me. She looks like she's just eaten something sour. Her brown eyes are narrowed into slits. Her nose is thin and stretched by the pull of her pursed lips. But then she looks at Ellis and transforms. Her face relaxes and the word 'beautiful' once again comes to my mind. Her pale skin radiates light against our bleak surroundings.

Adalyn takes the lead. She moves effortlessly over and around the fallen logs. She's so quick that it's almost impossible to follow her. My legs feel like they're made out of bags of sand.

"It's really important we keep up. Come on." Ellis tries to lift me up.

"Don't you have cars? Why do we have to walk?"

Ellis shakes his head. "All vehicles were banned a few years ago. A mandatory measure instituted by the Council to help curb the pollution."

"And you don't have anything else? You haven't invented a vehicle that runs without producing pollution?" I am shocked. A civilization that can travel to other planets can't come up with an eco-friendly mode of transportation?

"All resources have been devoted to reversing the damage we have caused Istriya. Adalyn heads the geological team studying ways to harness molten lava from the core of the planet and generate heat. It's been getting colder and colder on Istriya. Margaret's team is focused on maintaining the population. And another team is devoted to ensuring that all pollution-producing items are banned."

Adalyn stops and turns back to us. Her words whip out low and harsh. "Ellis, this is not the time for a history lesson. We need to move."

He leans forward again, arms outstretched.

"Don't. I can walk. If I'm holding you up, just go." I don't mean it, but the words come out anyway.

"I'm not going to leave you out here. We need to get to the base and speak to Lucas, the Council Leader. He's the only one who can help us. Time's running out." He holds out his arms, and this time I don't fight when he picks me up.

"Shh," Adalyn whispers when we catch up to her.

Ellis and I both look around. I can't see or hear anything.

"What? What is it?" asks Ellis.

"They're coming from over there, moving quickly." She glares at me. "We can't outrun them."

Her message is clear, but I'm not going to be the reason we get caught.

Meeting her glare, I say, "I'm slowing you down. You can move quicker without me." I push Ellis's arms away, but he tightens his hold. "I'll hide until they pass."

"Absolutely not! I'm not leaving you here by yourself."

"She has a point, Ellis ...."

"No!"

"Listen, you're still recovering. I'll take her. She won't slow me down at all. But we need to throw them off," Adalyn says.

"What are you suggesting?" Ellis asks, a strain in his voice.

"They're coming, Ellis. It's the only way I can think of. I'll take her, and we'll wait for you in my quarters."

Hang on. I'd be with her. And Ellis? He'd take them on by himself?

"That's stupid. Ellis can't distract and outrun them on his own. You said it yourself. He's still recovering, and he can't carry me either. I'm slowing him down." I wriggle to free myself from him. "So I'll hide, Ellis can head for the base, and you can create a diversion," I say pointedly. "And then once they're on the wrong path, you can come and get me, and we can meet Ellis at the base."

"Well, I guess that's an option too," Adalyn says with a grin. "You've found yourself yet another fan," she adds, raising her eyebrows.

"Kalli, you can't be left out here on your own—"

"But—"

"We don't have time to argue. We're going to follow Adalyn's plan," he says, passing me into her arms. "I'll be back with you soon," he promises.

I start to protest. He puts a finger to my lips. "Trust me."

He squeezes Adalyn's shoulder, and then he's gone.

"Okay, hang on." Adalyn breaks into a run.

I hold on to her tightly and curl into myself to prevent my limbs from whacking into the trees. Adalyn slows down, and I can see a large structure in the distance. She stops, and without setting me down, pulls out a thin blanket from her bag and drapes it over me.

"Just in case we run into someone, it's best if you stay hidden."

"Wh—"

"Shh. We're almost there and then you can talk. Just wait."

I can't see much through the blanket. There's little light from the sky, so under the blanket it's practically black. It feels like we're going down stairs. Something creaks. Her footsteps echo as we continue traveling down. At last she stops and places me on the ground. I free myself from the blanket. It doesn't take long for my eyes to adjust. The room is almost dark, except for a thin ray of light coming through a small window. Adalyn's standing on the other side of a door made of bars. Bars are all around. I'm in a jail cell.

"What are you doing? Where are we?"

Adalyn stares at me.

"Hey! Let me out of here," I say, getting up and pulling unsuccessfully on the locked door. "We're supposed to meet Ellis. You told him you were taking me to your place."

"Yeah, well, I took a slight detour. It's a little more private down here," she says, running her long fingers across the bars. "So exactly what are you going to tell the Council?"

"What? I don't know—"

"That's why you're here, right? To talk to the Council Leaders? To talk to Lucas." She paces uneasily back and forth. "What makes you think they'll listen to you? What do you know that would make them care? I've been trying to warn them about changes I have seen in the deeper caverns. But they just dismiss me. All they care about is finding an alternate heat source. They'll wish they had listened to me."

Hairs rise on the back of my neck. I have no idea what she's talking about. "I think Ellis will do most of the talking," I say, hoping that hearing his name will soothe her.

Despite being a few inches taller than Adalyn, I feel small under her stony gaze. I move closer to the bars, placing myself directly across from her. I steady my quivering legs and straighten my shoulders, so that when she looks at my face, she has to look up.

"I thought Ellis contacted you before we landed. Didn't he tell you everything that happened?"

"No, he did not. He just said that he was coming back and no one could know, and he had to speak with the Council." She crosses her arms. "So you will have to fill me in."

I slowly exhale and, as clearly as possible, I tell her how I accidently discovered the workshop and the photos. I give

173

a glossed-over version of the encounter that left Margaret with the silver rod embedded in her chest.

"Fallon plunged the bio-knife into Margaret?" Adalyn interrupts, her eyes wide in disbelief.

I swallow hard before continuing. My throat is parched and my voice barely audible.

I nod. "Ellis and Fallon realized that Margaret had no intention of honoring her promise not to harm the women they had used." I pause again to steady myself as my mind fills with vivid images of the women slumped in the glowing tanks. "They knew the Leaders would be against the brutality, so—"

"So they went against Margaret!" Her face presses against the bars as her hands wrap around them, shaking them violently. I jump away at the loud sound. Adalyn's eyes are glued on me. She takes a couple of steps back from the bars and leans against the rock wall. "Do you know why they were there? What those women were being used for?" she asks, scratching her long nails against the rocks, like nails on a chalkboard. I tense at the sound.

"Yes, I do."

She tilts her head, daring me to continue.

"The women were implanted with embryos from women on your planet."

My voice falters, and despite my intention not to, I glance down at my own stomach. It's brief, just a mere flick of my eyelids, but she catches it and pounces.

"You were Ellis's assignment, right?"

Assignment? The word drives a knife through my chest.

"Yes, I was," I say, my eyes glued to my hands.

"And what happened to your embryo? Was she placed in the tank? Where is the baby?" She rams back into the bars. "She wasn't on the ship with you?" she shrieks.

Baby? The word makes my stomach knot.

"No, we didn't bring the tank with us. Fallon said they weren't ready to move."

"Oh," she breathes, as she slumps down to the ground, her hands gripping the bars for support. "Okay, good. So she's in the tank? Fallon stayed behind to make sure everyone was fine?"

"Uh-huh." I shrug.

Adalyn slowly rises. She regards me critically. Before she even opens the door, I back away. She's fast. I've only taken two steps when she grabs my arm and yanks me to face her.

"Tell me the truth," she demands, her voice icy cold.

"Y-yes, Fallon stayed behind," I stutter.

"And the baby that was inside you, where is she?" She's so close to me that I feel her breath on my face.

I struggle to break from her grip.

"Tell me the truth!" she shrieks again.

"I was injured when they implanted me." I don't want to go on. I know why she's asking. I know I should lie to keep her calm and her rage in control. But the words are out before I can stop them. "I'm sorry. She didn't survive."

She looks at me, her eyes red. A sound of such immense anguish bellows from her that, the instant she releases me, I fall to my knees and cover my ears.

175

TWENTY-FOUR

Adalyn is curled up, sobbing on the ground. Her grief is all that exists in this room. It is so immense. I can feel it trying to swallow me up too. For an instant, I'm torn between escaping through the door she's left open and consoling her. I choose the door.

There's a tiny hallway, no more than four feet long. The walls and floor are made of roughened concrete. At the end of the corridor are two stairwells. One's slightly brighter than the other, so I opt for that one. I force my aching legs to run up the steps, taking two at a time. I stagger slightly at the top step, and I'm almost out when she grabs me and pulls me down.

Adalyn drags me back to the cell and flings me inside, slamming the door shut, sealing me in again. She sits on the other side of the bars, cross-legged, her back against the rocky wall.

"So you killed my baby." Her voice is even, her face blank. Not a single trace of her sorrow remains. She's even more frightening. "You said you were hurt when Ellis found you. What happened?"

Adalyn stares, waiting. With her long, multicolored hair draping her slender shoulders, she could be beautiful.

But there's something in her eyes that hardens her entire face and washes away her beauty. She's calmer than before, but I know her fury is rumbling just beneath the surface. I take a deep breath and carefully answer.

"I was in an alley. There was a guy there."

"A guy? What guy?"

"I didn't know him. He attacked me."

"Why? What did you do to him?" Her anger bubbles over.

I shake my head. "Nothing. He just attacked me. I think he would have killed me if Ellis hadn't come by and saved me."

"Oh yes, Ellis. We girls can always count on Ellis to save us." Her lips press into a tight line. "And then what happened? He took you to see Margaret?"

"Yes. She patched me back up."

"Did she give you some medicine to put on your stomach?"

I nod.

"And did you?" Her voice rises, as mine trembles.

"Yes, I did exactly what she told me to."

"Then I don't understand. What happened to the baby? If Margaret healed you and implanted my baby inside you, then she must have thought you were strong enough. What did you do?"

Adalyn is back on her feet, gripping the bars once again.

"I don't know what happened. I was going for a walk and Fallon found me. He got angry. He was pulling me back to Ellis's house and then ... and then." I pause and glance up, expecting to see maniacal eyes staring back at me, but Adalyn's expression is vacant.

"And," I press on, unsure if she's even listening anymore. "I was bleeding. Fallon and Ellis tried to help. Margaret showed up, but she refused to help."

"She refused? Why would she refuse? This was all her idea! Her mastermind plan to save our people."

I have no choice but to tell her the truth. "Margaret said that I was just an extra. She had enough embryos collected and didn't need the one inside me."

Adalyn crumples to the ground.

"Fallon and Ellis tried to save the embryo, the baby." I cringe at the thought of an actual baby being inside me. "But they couldn't."

The last of my words are drowned out by an agonizing moan. It starts low and grows until everything in the room buckles from the weight of the pain pouring out of Adalyn.

"I'm sorry," I whisper.

We sit there for what feels like hours, on either side of the door. Adalyn is motionless. Her body folds over so that her face is pressed into her knees.

Eventually she straightens up and regards me with an empty expression. She rises, opens the door, and walks toward me.

"Just one more question. Who wanted to save the baby? Ellis or Fallon?"

"Both of them did. They both wanted to."

"Okay then, let's go."

She pulls out a vial that hangs from a chain around

her neck. It's similar to the one Ellis gave me. Adalyn pops open the lid and a soft blue light emanates from it. She puts her lips to the vial like she's going to drink from it, but instead she murmurs quietly and then seals it back up.

She grabs my hand when we reach the top of the steps.

"You were hidden on the way in, but I want you to see what it looks like before I cover you back up."

Still holding my hand, she leads me through the door. Gray is the prevalent color, or lack of color. The sky is dull. The ground is brown dirt intermixed with dirty white stones.

"It's so ugly, isn't it? And cold." She rubs her hands up and down her arms. "It wasn't always like this. Even I can remember when the ground was green and the light from our sun was able to penetrate the thick fog." She breathes in deeply and swings her brightly colored hair. "They should have listened to me. But now they will."

She walks over to a wooden box, opens it, and pulls out the blanket, along with something that resembles a metal ruler with a drill bit on one end. She folds the ruler over so that it fits into her jacket pocket, and comes toward me with the blanket.

"Wait. What are you doing? I thought you said I could see."

"And you did. But now it's time to get going."

"Are we going to meet Ellis?"

"Ellis?" She pulls out the vial from within her shirt. It's now glowing a deep orange. "Yes, that's exactly where we're going."

She throws the blanket over me, and I push it off.

"Why do I have to wear this?"

"Because we don't want anyone to see you before I'm ready," Adalyn says, as she readjusts the covering.

We're moving quickly again. Adalyn keeps muttering to herself. When she finally speaks, her words are neither angry nor flat, but filled with sadness.

"I am sorry about all those women. I never wanted any part of this plan. I didn't think it was the right thing to do."

I push away at the top of the blanket so that I can see her face. I expect her to immediately cover me back up, but she doesn't. Tears are flowing down her cheeks.

"Adalyn, are we still going to meet Ellis?" I take in as much of my surroundings as I can before I'm concealed again.

The sky is a blanket of gray stretching all around. Adalyn looks at me as if she's startled by my presence.

"Not yet time for you to make your appearance."

She covers me up.

"Please, Adalyn," I beg. "Can you at least tell me if we are still going to meet Ellis?"

"Yes, of course. That's exactly where I'm taking you. We should move a little faster though. They're gathering right now."

I feel a tiny surge of hope. Maybe she's going to actually help. Her reaction to the loss of her child, though frightening, was normal. And her animosity toward me has passed. She's taking me to meet Ellis. This could all still work out. I settle loosely into her arms and allow the waves of hope and optimism to wash over me.

TWENTY-FIVE

"Okay, Kalli, we're almost there." Adalyn slows down. "I want you to see something." She pulls the cloak off. "You can walk from here," she says, setting me on my feet.

I can only see about fifty feet in front of me. We're on a road, with fallen logs on either side.

"This was once the most beautiful place. I've seen pictures of what it was like. These were magnificent trees. Their top branches disappeared into the vapors."

"Vapors?"

"Sorry, you would call them clouds, I believe. The trees used to be adorned with flowers. Beautiful big flowers. And the colors …." She closes her eyes and inhales deeply. "The colors were more brilliant than you can even imagine. The ground … well, you'll see what I mean."

"What happened to it?"

"We happened." She opens her eyes. "Our greed. Our ignorance. My people destroyed our planet. They took and took until there was no more, and now this is what is left. Our atmosphere is so damaged that the sun can't reach us. I can't remember the last time I woke to a brightly lit day. Now the only color in my life are these ribbons in

181

my hair. Come on, we're almost there."

My insides bristle. It feels like so much time has passed since I left Earth. Will Navi still be okay? Will Margaret go after him, like she did Sammy? I need to speak with Ellis. He would know. He would have figured a way to contact Fallon.

"Will Ellis be waiting for us?

Adalyn doesn't answer but instead she nods in front of her. I strain my eyes to see what she's looking at.

"It's beautiful isn't it?" she asks.

It? And then I see what she sees. The ground has softened and there's a gentle breeze blowing. The gray mist thins and I can see out farther. Suddenly, there's a burst of orange and red popping out against the dreary backdrop. Beautiful flowers dangle from the trees. My nose awakens. There's a sweet smell in the air. I take a deep breath.

I feel something touch my leg and glance down. Long willowy grass, intermixed with flowers of pinks, blues, and yellows. Adalyn bends down and gently touches one.

"Hurry, Kalli. They'll be here soon. I want you to see this before."

I run to catch up to her. "Before wh—?" And then I stop cold.

Massive trees crowned with sparse green foliage are rooted at the base of a one-hundred-foot-high rocky cliff. A waterfall cascades down the center of the cliff, splashing onto stones and trailing away as a stream.

"This is what most of Istriya once looked like," Adalyn says softly. "And now this is all we have left."

She grabs hold of my hand. At her touch, the hairs on the back of my neck spring up, and I pull my hand away.

"I thought Ellis was going to be here. You said we were going to meet him," I say.

"They'll be here soon. I just wanted you to see for yourself, before it got crazy. Soon this will be gone too. But it doesn't matter anymore," Adalyn says, her eyes on my belly. And then looking beyond me, she adds, "Perfect timing."

I turn in the direction Adalyn is looking and see shapes coming out of the mist. A wall of men and women swell toward us. The explosion of color takes my breath away. They are draped in bright blue and orange and yellow and green. The group closest to us is covered in the most brilliant attire. Shiny red cloaks edged with a thick purple fringe. Amongst this group, a tall slender man, with silver hair as thin as mist, wearing a golden crown, moves ahead of everyone.

My stomach lurches. Who are these people? The Council? Where's Ellis?

"Adalyn, what is the meaning of this? What is the emergency you summoned us to?" demands the man with the crown.

Adalyn bows deeply in front of him. But before she has a chance to respond a voice pierces the air.

"I would like to know the same thing."

All heads turn to find the source of the voice. My legs buckle and my breathing quickens at the sight of Margaret gripping Fallon. We took too long.

"Margaret. Fallon," Adalyn says, quickly standing upright.

Margaret glares at me.

"Hello, Kalli," she says, her voice tight. "Thought you could turn someone else against me?"

Fear has gripped my vocal chords, and I'm unable to respond. I look at Fallon. His face is swollen. What has she done to him?

"It's not what you think," says Adalyn.

"Enough!" comes the deep voice of the Leader.

The crowd, including Margaret, bows.

"What is the meaning of all of this? Margaret, why have you returned? Why did you contact the guards to take hold of spaceship D20?"

Margaret throws Fallon at the feet of the Leader.

"The mission has been compromised. Ellis and Fallon tried to sabotage the removal of the embryos from the subjects. They are guilty of the ultimate crime."

Gasps emit from all around.

"Ellis and Fallon? I don't understand. They have been committed to this mission from the start. Where is Ellis?"

"He fled with her on D20," Margaret says, as all eyes follow hers and turn to me.

The crowd has a collective intake of breath, followed by a smattering of nervous chatter. My skin feels clammy. A slight moan escapes my lips, and Fallon's eyes meet mine.

The Leader looks from Margaret to Fallon to Adalyn and then to me.

"Where is Ellis?" he asks, staring right at me.

I close my eyes. I can do this. I will do this. This is my

chance to explain what happened and save those women.

But before I can say anything, Adalyn interrupts, "Ellis will be here soon."

"Lucas—I mean, my Lord," interjects Margaret. "I must return and complete the project—"

"No!" I blurt out. Adalyn pierces her nails into my wrist, as I unsuccessfully try to pull away.

"Sorry for the outburst," Adalyn says, without looking at me. She shoves me behind her.

The Leader tilts his head slightly, a gesture strikingly similar to Ellis's.

"What is your name?" he asks me, his voice calm.

Adalyn digs her nails deeper into my skin. Why is she doing this?

"Adalyn, let go of her," commands the Leader. He returns his gaze to me, awaiting my answer.

I rub my wrist and blood spreads across my skin.

"My name is Kalli," I say, steadying my voice.

"And why are you here, Kalli?"

"My Lord," Margaret again interrupts, but the Leader holds up his hand to silence her. "You can't believe anything she says."

He glares at her, and Margaret submits. She bows and takes a step back.

"Why are you here, Kalli?" he repeats.

I pull my shoulders back and stand up straight and tall. "Margaret and her team lied," I begin.

"That is a serious accusation," he says.

"Yes, but it is true. I believe that Margaret promised

not to harm any of us on Earth, but she killed the initial surrogates, she killed a little boy, and now she is going to kill the remaining women after your embryos are removed." I still my shaking legs. I will not fail.

"Do you have any proof?" he asks.

"Of course there is no—"

"Margaret, be quiet. You will get your chance." He turns back to me. "Well, Kalli, where is your proof?"

Proof? Sammy's tortured body? Would that be proof?

"The proof is me," I say, my voice strong.

Margaret smirks. I refuse to allow her to belittle me. I'm not her victim anymore. I'm not anyone's victim. "She was going to kill me. The embryo inside me died." Beside me, Adalyn lets out a low moan, but I continue. "I was bleeding and Margaret wouldn't help me. She said that I knew too much. She couldn't erase my memory because the modifier doesn't work. She will kill all those women." Everything comes out in disjointed bursts.

The Leader inhales sharply. "Is there anyone who can support your accusations?"

"Yes, there are two people. Ellis and …." I look at Fallon and the Leader follows my gaze.

"Fallon?" he booms.

Fallon rises and bows. His face is pale and puffy.

"You have heard what Kalli has just said. Is it true? Are the subjects on Earth in danger? Has Margaret killed a child?"

Our eyes meet and then Fallon stares at his feet. He takes a deep breath as I hold mine. Will he tell the truth? It seems like forever before Fallon speaks, but when he does, it's barely audible.

"Fallon, I'm sure you realize the gravity of the situation. It is very important that the Council and I hear what you say," says the Leader.

Fallon opens his mouth again, but the voice that echoes through the crowd is not his.

"Let her go. Don't hurt her!" Ellis pushes his way through the crowd of people.

Margaret lunges to grab him, but Ellis maneuvers around her outstretched arms.

"Ellis," the Leader says, "are you all right?"

The genuine concern in the Leader's voice surprises me.

"Yes, my Lord, I am okay, but I need to tell you ...."

And then Ellis clearly and concisely tells the entire story. As he speaks, I look up at the Leader and see the doubt in his eyes turn to shock, and then anger. Once Ellis has finished, the Leader turns to Margaret but says nothing. He waits.

"It's not true. The mission is proceeding as I said it would. We have harvested hundreds of embryos. Soon they will be ready to implant into our own females. Our race will continue to survive. That was the only goal," Margaret says, her jaw set firmly.

The Leader regards Margaret, his eyes black and cold, his face hard.

"Did you harm the subjects? Did you kill a child?" he asks, his voice quiet but frightening.

"What? Harm them? We carried out the mission as we

had planned."

"The primary condition of the mission was that under no circumstances were the subjects to be harmed," the Leader says.

"Of course, every precaution was taken to ensure adherence to that condition, but in some instances, we ran into deviations that we had to address. You must understand that creating the mission on paper is not the same as actually doing it. There were unexpected situations. What would you have had me do? Tough choices had to be made, and I made them."

"You had no right! You should have consulted the Council. We make the decisions, not you. We decide what is best."

"And look where that has gotten us," Margaret says, raising her voice for the first time.

Murmurs of shock emit from the crowd. Margaret appears taller as she squares her shoulders and faces the Leader. Neither speaks. The Leader raises his eyebrows as he stares at Margaret. An uncomfortable silence passes, until it is broken by a low moan.

The sound grows louder. Heads turn, looking for the source. People direct their gaze toward me, but it's not coming from me. It's coming from Adalyn. She's on her knees. Sweat beads across her forehead, even though it's cold. Her hands are clenched around the ruler-like object. She repeatedly plunges the rod into the ground. Her eyes are shut, and she gives out one prolonged shriek followed by another. The ground beneath Adalyn rumbles and splits apart. The crack travels from Adalyn to the large circular stone that I'm standing beside. And then with an ear-splitting boom, the stone opens up into a monstrous pit of molten lava. Screams erupt around me.

"Adalyn!" several voices shout out.

Adalyn opens her eyes. She places the rod across the opening. Taking hold of my wrist, she walks toward the Leader and Margaret.

"Adalyn, what have you done?" the Leader demands.

"What have I done? What have all of you done? Or to be precise, not done? I told you that I'd discovered that the core of our planet has become unstable. The molten lava is rising up closer and closer to the surface. Very soon, our entire planet will be riddled with volcanoes and massive quakes. We will be smothered in scorching liquid. I came to you with all of this, and you did nothing. Instead, you listened to her." She glares at Margaret. "How could you think that bringing babies into this world would solve anything?"

"Adalyn. That's enough," demands Margaret.

Adalyn glances at Margaret and then Fallon. "I told you I didn't want to do it. I begged you, Fallon," Adalyn says. "I told you it wasn't safe to bring a child into the world. I told you I wanted to make it better here first. I told you about the caverns. I showed you all my research. But even you refused to listen. You only listened to her!" Adalyn is shrieking and sobbing.

"Please, Addy," Fallon begs.

"She killed my baby! You allowed it to happen. My

baby! In spite of everything, I loved her. And you put my baby into this." Adalyn waves me in front of Fallon. "Kalli told me everything. How she was damaged before the implantation. How she was an extra. And you still put my baby inside her. You gambled away the life of my baby."

"I'm sorry. I'm so sorry," he says, moving toward her.

I tear my eyes away from Adalyn and search for Ellis, but I can't see him.

"Now you're sorry? Well, it's too late. I told you the problem we're facing isn't going to be solved by having babies. Our planet is dying. Did you hear any sounds in the forest? Anything?" She pulls me closer to the opening. "No, you didn't hear anything, because nothing lives there anymore. Everything has died. We have poisoned our planet. We have used and taken until there is nothing left. We can't have children because our planet is toxic. Molten rock has risen into the caverns beneath us, and you refuse to listen, refuse to do anything about it. And the solution you come up with is to have babies? And you forced me to be part of it." She turns abruptly to face Margaret, her words soaked with venom. "You forced me to fall in love with that baby, and then you took her away from me."

"What are you doing, Addy? Let go of Kalli and move away from the chamber. This isn't part of the plan." It's Ellis. He's standing directly in front of us. My body pulls toward him and safety. He's so close.

"Sometimes even you can be a bit slow, Ellis. The plan has changed."

"What do you mean? We're all here. The Council

knows what's actually happening on Earth. Those women will be saved. Kalli will be saved."

"Is that all you care about? Kalli? What about me? What about the baby? Your baby!" Her words hit me harder than her fists.

"What are you talking about, Addy?" he asks, his eyes wild. "The baby was yours and Fallon's. Why would you make up such a painful lie?"

"I'm not lying about anything. Don't you remember all those late nights we'd stay up trying to figure out how to fix all of this? Don't you remember what we did? We didn't just talk."

Ellis shakes his head and runs his fingers through his hair.

"You bastard!" Fallon explodes and charges toward Ellis. But the Leader holds him back.

Ensnaring Fallon in his arms, the Leader says, "Enough! You have completely disgraced our family."

"Disgrace? That's all you care about? I lost my baby!" Adalyn storms.

"Adalyn, stop lying. That never happened. Yes, we talked. You're like a sister to me. You were going to marry my brother. I would never—"

"But you did. You must remember. That night when you found out you were chosen to be a Keeper. You were so confused. You didn't know if you wanted to do it. And I told you I didn't think it was right to bring children into our world and we stayed up all night talking and ...."

"No." Ellis's voice is barely a whisper.

"I've always loved you, Ellis. It was always supposed to be you and me. But instead you went and fell for her," she says, shoving me toward him.

Ellis reaches out to grab me, but she yanks me back so hard that we teeter over the edge.

"Adalyn, be careful," Ellis cries.

"Be careful with what? Me or her?"

"Please, Addy," Fallon says.

"Adalyn, enough of this! I don't know what is going on between you and my sons, but I want you to move away from the chamber and unhand that girl right now!" demands the Leader.

Sons? So this is Ellis's father. The Leader of the planet? Lucas?

"I agree. Enough of this." Adalyn turns to face the crowd. "Our planet is dying. We can't have any more children. None of you listened to me. And now my baby is dead! I can't take anymore of this. I won't." She's sobbing. Her body shakes as we both teeter on the edge of the fiery pit.

Oh God! She's going to take me with her. I pull away, and Adalyn and I lose our balance. Ellis and Fallon rush forward. Ellis reaches out to grab me at the exact instant Fallon's hands wrap around my waist and pull me back. Ellis's hands pass over my arms as he and Adalyn disappear into the flaming cavern. I lunge to grab him back, but I'm too late. The rod that Adalyn placed in the opening snaps and the chamber reseals itself, trapping Ellis within its fiery hold. I scream out his name, even though I know my voice will never reach him.

192

TWENTY-SIX

People shout and run in all directions. Many fall and are lost beneath the rush of pounding feet. A spark shoots out, and the sky is filled with a shower of lights, a cascade of falling fireworks. The Leader and the other Council members have their arms raised to the air. Each is holding a vial similar to the one Ellis gave me. Everyone stops.

Ellis's father drops to his knees, staring at the stone that has claimed Ellis and Adalyn. Margaret clutches her chest, her eyes fixed on the stone. Fallon has his arms wrapped around me, holding me back as I struggle to break free.

Finally someone speaks. His voice echoes through the crowd. He instructs everyone to return to their homes and await further instructions. He insists the departure be done in an orderly manner. He then informs the remaining Council members to escort Margaret, Fallon, and me back to Head Lodgings.

I can't move. Ellis is gone. Someone holds a hand out to me. I look up. It's the Leader, Ellis's father.

"Kalli, I would like you to come back to the main house with me."

I shake my head. I'm not leaving Ellis. He's down there.

I have to get him out. I shove Fallon away and claw into the dirt and rock.

"It won't work. The chamber has sealed itself. We can't get in this way."

"You're not even trying! He's down there, burning alive. How can you just give up on your own son?" My words come out in sobs.

"I have not given up on Ellis. But I don't think he would be happy with me if I left you here either. You obviously meant something to my son. He risked the entire mission for you. And now he just ...."

I choke back a sob. I know exactly what Ellis has just done for me. I look at Ellis's father, his face ashen. The strength that existed when he first arrived has vanished.

"Kalli, we have to go now," Fallon says, his voice hollow.

Fallon's loss is so great it has consumed him. His hand trembles as he reaches out for me, and I take it. He pulls me up, and we slowly walk away. I turn to see Ellis's father kneeling by the chamber, his hands placed on the exact spot where his son was claimed.

"Lucas? My Lord?" Fallon calls out softly.

Slowly Lucas rises and follows us. We make our way along the same path Adalyn and I had taken. This time the burst of colors have no effect on me. I'm unable to appreciate their beauty when my heart hurts so much. He can't be dead. Tears fall down my cheeks.

Lucas passes us, squeezing Fallon's shoulder as he walks on.

"Adalyn was too fragile," Fallon says.

"We will sort it all out, Fallon," Lucas says. "We need to move faster. They are waiting for us. If we have a chance of settling all of this, it must be done quickly. Are you strong enough or should I?" he asks, nodding toward me.

"No, I can do it," Fallon says and then turns to me. "Kalli, may I?" He holds his arms open. For the first time, he isn't commanding but asking.

I nod. Fallon collects me into his arms. He looks so unbelievably tired. I'm shocked that he's still able to travel at such a fantastic speed. I wrap my arms around his neck as he sprints back through the lifeless forest.

Fallon places me carefully back on my feet. We stand in front of two towering steel gates stretching thirty feet high. Guards, dressed in white jackets with shiny silver buttons, push open the gates and bow to Lucas as he passes through. Fallon takes my hand and ushers me along.

The building is a palace with marble columns and balconies. The exterior of the structure glistens as if crystals are embedded in it. Lucas has already disappeared through the wooden doors.

People rush about, speaking in hushed tones, when the quiet urgency is broken by a piercing shriek.

"There she is!" Margaret lunges for me, but Fallon holds her back. "Let me go, Fallon! How dare you bring her here? Into my home! She should be taken to the cells."

"Margaret, stop. Lucas asked her to come."

"That's right, I did." Lucas suddenly appears. "Fallon, take Kalli to the kitchen, and then meet me in my office."

"Absolutely not! I won't have it," Margaret says, grabbing

on to Lucas's arm, "How dare you? She killed our son." Pain rips through my chest, and I stumble at the thought of Ellis dying.

"How can you say such a thing? You were there. You saw what happened to Ellis." Lucas yanks his arm away from her.

Margaret continues her tirade. "She has destroyed everything."

"I'm not certain it was Kalli who put us in this position," he says, his eyes narrowing. "Fallon, I'll be waiting for you."

"Oh, I've got to hear this." Margaret crosses her arms.

"No, Margaret. Kartac will escort you to the study."

"Escort me? This is my home, Lucas. I will go wherever I please."

Lucas's face stiffens and his nostrils flare. "You will go with Kartac, or perhaps you would prefer Weston?"

Fallon lets out a tiny gasp. Margaret's expression morphs into fear. "You wouldn't," she breathes.

Lucas raises his eyebrows. Margaret turns and marches down the hallway. A man, who I can only assume is Kartac, solemnly follows.

"I'll be right back, Father," Fallon says. He takes my arm, and we move along the corridor in Margaret's stormy wake.

"Kalli, you can wait here." Fallon's face has completely altered. All traces of hostility have disappeared and have been replaced with grief. "Stay here with Waverly. I'll be back soon," he says, squeezing my arm.

"We have to find Ellis. Can't we look for him first, and

then you can talk to Lucas?"

For some unknown reason, my body acts on its own volition, and my hand reaches out to Fallon. He takes hold of it. Our eyes lock, and I know he shares my pain.

"I'll be right back," he whispers.

Waverly darts around the massive kitchen, stealing glances at me. She's tiny in every way. Her tight curls jiggle as she scoots around the kitchen. She silently lays out a plate of food in front of me. I can't recognize anything. It doesn't matter. I'm not hungry. All I can think about is saving Ellis.

The weight of the realization disorients me. I would have been the first to call someone who could forgive such treachery a fool. Ellis lied to me. Am I only forgiving him because he may be dead?

I startle at the sudden pressure on my back.

"Let's go." Fallon holds out his hand, and I take it, relieved that we're going to find Ellis.

"Have they found him? Is there a chance?" I choke out the last bit.

Fallon doesn't answer. He moves quickly, his eyes darting around.

"Fallon," I breathe heavily, almost running to keep up with his long strides. "Is Ellis okay? Has anyone found him?"

Still no response.

"Fallon, you have to tell me. Is he—is he … gone?"

Fallon draws me in behind a corner. He speaks in a hushed and hurried manner. "We need to move quickly. I will tell you everything as soon as we're outside. Trust me,

Kalli. Please."

I nod, and Fallon pulls me along again. Others are rushing around too, some giving out commands. If any of the instructions are meant for us, Fallon ignores them and trudges on.

Finally we're outside again, and I turn to him, expecting him to explain. Hoping against hope that he'll tell me that Ellis has been found and is okay. But Fallon just meets my desperate eyes with a quick shake of his head.

"Not yet. We're almost there," he says, moving so fast he's practically running.

He drags me along, and I almost fall. Fallon wraps his arm around my waist, lifting my feet from the ground, and runs. We're heading toward a white marble structure. It's huge, at least forty feet high and almost as wide. He pulls me down into a crouch. His face is inches from mine, and I can see the swelling under his eyes.

"Things are moving very quickly," Fallon whispers. "Lucas may not be in power much longer."

"What?" I ask a little too loudly, and Fallon covers my mouth with his hand.

"Shhh," he warns, and then continues on. "Our planet has been suffering for a long time. People were already losing faith in Lucas's ability to lead us through this crisis, and now the mission failed under his watch. Plus all that stuff Adalyn said, about the Council not listening to her warnings, has cast a dark mark upon Lucas. Having a Leader who can be looked up to and trusted is critical. Lucas has been told that there are many in the Council who want him replaced."

This doesn't matter now. "What about Ellis?" I breathe, trying to keep my voice as quiet as possible.

"I'm getting to that," he hisses. "Lucas's time in power may be ending soon. We need to act quickly." He grips my shoulders so that we're looking at each other straight on. "We can try and save Ellis and Adalyn, or I can take you back to Earth. Lucas can get us a ship, and we can leave."

"What are you talking about? Of course I want to save Ellis. Why would we leave?"

"When Adalyn opened the chamber, she destabilized Istriya's core. The catastrophes she warned us about are going to happen. And happen soon. Lucas has people trying to counter it, but there's no certainty that they will be successful." He bites his lower lip. I look at him, waiting. "If they can't, then Istriya will be destroyed."

"What? That's crazy!"

"Lucas can get us a ship. I can get you back to Earth."

"Then why isn't everyone freaking out? Trying to escape?"

He raises his eyebrows and tilts his head.

And then it hits me. "They don't know."

"There aren't enough ships to get everyone off the planet. The Council ruled that in the interest of public safety—"

"Public safety? But everyone will die!"

"Kalli, it would be chaos if everyone found out. Anyway, it's not up to us. The Council has made a decision to announce that the situation is under control."

"And they'll let me go? Aren't they worried that I'd talk and tell people about what you did?"

"The Council isn't going to stop you from leaving Istriya," Fallon says.

"You didn't answer my question."

"I did. You will be safe. Your brother will be safe."

I shake my head. "Margaret was going to kill me and all those women because she couldn't modify our memories."

"Margaret isn't in charge. Kalli, you need to decide. We don't have much time."

Even after everything Ellis has done—the deceit, the heartache—I can't leave without trying to save him. I look down at the thin dark line on my arm. A scar is already forming along the spot where Fallon removed the verbindi. It wasn't all a lie. It couldn't have been. Ellis risked his own life to save mine. "I want to find him."

Fallon shakes his head and laughs. "You two are so alike. Wanting to save everyone. Thinking you can. It's not going to end how you think. It's not going to be happily ever after for you and Ellis."

"Don't you think I know that?"

"I don't get it. You've only known him seven days. He lied to you. Deceived you. Endangered your life. How can you forgive someone like that?" He turns away from me and mutters, "How can Addy love someone like that?"

Pretending I didn't hear the last part, I say. "I know it makes me look like an idiot. But I don't think forgiving someone makes me weak. I think it's a sign of strength. And I forgive him."

"But how? Was your life so miserable that you fall for the first person who shows you a little compassion?"

I inhale sharply. His words sting.

"I'm sorry. I shouldn't have said that," he says.

"It's true. My life was miserable, but I'm not a fool. I know what he did. And I hated him for it. I probably still do. But I can't pretend that I don't love him. Even after you removed the verbindi, I still had feelings for him." I cross my arms over my chest.

"I don't get it."

"I know." I smile at him. "After all the crap I've had to deal with, I never thought I'd feel for someone the way I feel about Ellis. I thought that Sita and her men had taken away my ability to trust, to love. But they didn't. That means something to me. It's something to fight for. It's something I deserve."

Fallon takes my hand. "Okay, Kalli, let's go."

TWENTY-SEVEN

Fallon peers over the edge of the structure.

"It's clear. But we have to move quickly."

The scenery whips by in shades of gray and brown. Ellis's voice plays out in my head. *The home I grew up in was very bleak. I hated it.* According to Adalyn, this was once a beautiful planet, full of plants and animals and vibrant life. How could they allow this to happen? Margaret said humans destroyed everything we touched. Is this the future that awaits us?

Fallon slows down and walks between two large, barren trees. He sets me down and brushes away the dirt. I move to help him, but he holds up his hand.

"Stand back. Addy told me that somewhere in here is an ancient entrance to a cavern system she discovered when she was mapping the planet's crust. Ah! I think this might be it."

Fallon grabs a stick and draws a circle around the clearing. He digs his hands in and pulls. His neck, shoulders, and arms bulge under the strain. With a guttural yell, he removes a large disk of solid rock, revealing a dark gaping hole about three feet wide. Fallon collapses next to the massive stone, gasping and coughing.

"Are you okay?" I ask.

"Yeah, fine," he croaks and stiffly gets back up. "You understand, Kalli, that once we go down there and start looking for Ellis and Addy, I can't guarantee having enough time to get you off the planet before ...." The ground shifts beneath our feet. He doesn't finish. He doesn't have to.

The shiver that runs through me has nothing to do with the cold temperature. "I understand. I want to find Ellis."

I was prepared to die when Ellis and I walked into the workshop, and then again when we jumped off the ship. I'm still prepared.

He reaches under his shirt and pulls out a black pouch. He unzips the flap and removes a tiny flask. "Take a sip, you're going to need the energy. I bet you haven't eaten all day."

I think back to the last time I had eaten. I woke this morning to a note from Ellis saying he had gone out for hot chocolate. That seems a lifetime ago. I take the flask and drink the cool liquid that wets my cracked lips and parched throat.

"Hey, not too much. Your body's not used to this stuff."

"What is it?"

"It's called Reponera. It quenches thirst and energizes the body. It even has a few healing properties." He returns the flask into the pouch. "Okay, let's get down there."

Fallon grabs a thick branch. "Get on my back and hold on tightly." And stressing each word, he says, "Do not let go."

Fallon stoops down so I can climb onto his back. He places the stick inside the hole, wedging it against the walls.

"Okay, hang on. The first step is the bumpiest."

I squeeze my arms and legs as tight as I can around Fallon's body. He leans over and grasps the branch, and we slide into the hole. I scream as I hear the stick cracking under our weight, but the expected plunge never comes. Fallon wedges his feet into the sides of the walls, holding us in place. Using the broken stick and his feet, he inches us down the dark pit until his feet hit solid ground.

"Kalli," he squeaks. "You can let go."

He clicks on a tiny flashlight, and I can see red blotches on his neck.

"Sorry about that," I say.

"Don't worry about it. Come on." He grabs my hand.

We creep along the narrow passage, his flashlight casting eerie shadows along the rocky walls. I squeeze his hand reflexively and feel his fingers tighten in response. The air is parched in the cramped tunnel. My breath comes in short sharp gasps.

"Do you really think there's a chance he survived?" I ask.

"Addy said there are places to hide from the smoke and flames. Ellis is strong, Kalli."

"He's not." My voice quivers. "His parachute didn't open. I thought he was dead. But Adalyn did something. I don't know if it worked." I clasp my hands and press them against my lips.

"Kalli." Fallon pulls my hands from my face and unclenches my fingers. "We are going to find them."

"How do you know that?"

"Because she can't be dead. Not like this." For an instant, I see a man who has lost everything. His entire face pulled down from the weight of his grief. But just as quickly, Fallon recovers. The sadness is replaced with determination. He straightens. "We need to keep going. Addy had mapped out all these caverns. She showed me once, so I know how to get to the main cavern. The temperature is going to get even more intense but as long as we stay on the path we'll be okay. The drink you had, the Reponera, will keep you hydrated, but you really have to slow down your breathing."

We walk along for what seems like hours, the only sound our footsteps crunching in the rubble. Fallon's flashlight provides a narrow stream of light along our path, leaving the rest of our surroundings completely hidden. My imagination spirals to visions of poisonous creatures slithering nearby, waiting to strike.

"Do you know how much farther?" I ask.

"I've been counting the turns we've made. We should be coming to a fork soon. We keep to the left and once we hear the roaring of the lava, we'll be close to the spot Ellis and Adalyn fell."

And he's right. Just when I think my legs are about to fail, we arrive at the fork, and my energy rebounds.

"We stay to the left," he says and pulls me along that way.

Within seconds, the intensity of the heat soars. I'm drenched in sweat. It's running down my face, blurring my already poor vision. My ears ring at the deafening roar.

"Stay close," Fallon shouts. "We're almost there. Start

yelling and looking for them."

I scream out Ellis's name over the sound of the fire that looms ahead.

It starts as an orange glow casting light upon our feet. As we move closer, the fire swells into a blinding blaze that emerges from the middle of the large cavern.

"Stay against the walls, Kalli," Fallon says.

He pushes his foot out slowly, prodding the ground for stability. At about three feet, it cracks and splinters. I plaster myself against the wall as we move around the fiery pit.

Sparks shoot out. Fallon tries to shield me. I duck my head out from behind him, trying to see through the flames.

A movement to my left catches my eye a second before Fallon notices. It's a body, about twenty feet from me. Ellis. I run toward him. Fallon reaches out to grab me but misses. I'm only a few feet from Ellis, when I see the long rainbow streaked hair. Adalyn. Her arm is outstretched toward Ellis's hand. With only inches remaining, they hadn't succeeded in closing the gap.

I grab Ellis's arm and pull. His eyes open, and then suddenly, I feel the ground beneath us giving way.

TWENTY-EIGHT

"No, Kalli. Go back," Ellis breathes.

Before I can answer, I'm torn from Ellis and flung against the wall.

"Ellis," I cry, crawling back to him.

Something suddenly lands with an echoing thud on my right. I turn to see Ellis slumped beside me, and Fallon, blackened and glistening with sweat, beside him. The ground Ellis had been lying on just seconds before breaks into a thousand pieces and plummets into the fire.

Gasping, Fallon looks at me. "You are such an idiot."

"Where's Adalyn?" I ask, afraid of the answer.

Fallon jerks his head to my left, and there, lying on her back, with her arms and legs splayed, is Adalyn. Fallon tugs at the zipper on his pack and removes the flask. He pours the liquid into Ellis's mouth. And then he crawls over to Adalyn, cradles her in his arms, and gives her a drink too.

"Kalli," Ellis moans softly beside me.

I lift his head onto my lap. I can't believe it. He's here with me. We're together. We're alive. His hand reaches up and touches my face.

"You found me," he croaks. "How?"

"Fallon," I whisper back.

207

He smiles and nods. Fallon is back on his feet, carrying Adalyn's limp body.

"Is she—?"

"She's alive," Fallon says. "Are you able to walk?" he asks Ellis.

Ellis nods, and together we clamber to our feet. With our arms entwined around each other, we follow Fallon along the edge of the cavern and back into the darker corridor.

Ellis draws me closer into his body. "When I first saw you, I thought I was hallucinating. A beautiful memory to take with me," he says. "After all I've done, you still came. Why?"

Even in the absence of light, I can see his eyes fixed to mine. Those eyes that I had fallen for the instant I had seen them. Those eyes that had stared into mine and lied. Those eyes that I hated. But now I finally look past all of that and see what's really there.

"Because I couldn't allow another catastrophe to shape my life. You made mistakes. Terrible mistakes. But I believe that a lot of what you did was out of love. Love for your people and then love for me. And I thought you deserved a chance. That we both deserve a chance."

"Thank you, Kalli."

"We don't have time for this, Ellis," Fallon says. "We have to get to the ships."

"So what's the plan, Fallon?" Ellis asks.

"Lucas doesn't think he's going to be in power much longer. And considering everything that happened …." His gaze drops to Adalyn for a split second and then quickly resumes looking ahead. "He's probably right. Like I told Kalli, there's no guarantee we can make it to the ships to get off Istriya."

"Why the hurry?"

"It's because of what I did," Adalyn says.

We all look at her, shocked at the sound of her voice.

"It's my fault. Isn't it?" Adalyn presses.

None of us answer. But there is a response. It starts with a slow grumble and then escalates as the ceiling implodes and massive pieces of jagged rock come crashing down.

Ellis pins me against the wall, shielding me, as the air fills with endless echoes of deafening crashes.

It's happening. The disasters Adalyn warned about are happening. It's so loud it hurts.

Then as quickly as it started, it stops. The roaring ceases and is replaced by something even worse. A cry so painful and shrill, my ribs vibrate inside my chest.

"Kalli, are you okay?" Ellis breathes into my ears.

"Yes," I croak.

It is no longer dark. The black cavernous roof has been replaced by a gray lifeless sky. And in this dismal source of light, I can see the enormity of the devastation. Massive rocks and rubble surround us. Our bodies, faces, and hair coated in dust. And on top of the rubble is Adalyn. A tortured sound escapes her lips. At first I think she's trapped, but then I notice her arms rising and plunging back into the rocks, throwing them aside.

"Fallon," she cries. "I'm so sorry, Fallon."

"Oh my God!" Ellis says. "Adalyn, where's Fallon?"

She screams as she heaves a huge boulder from below her. "I don't know. He threw me aside and then he fell and everything came crashing down."

"Kalli, stay right here. Don't move."

Ellis crawls over to Adalyn and starts moving aside the rocks.

"He risked his life for me!" Adalyn sobs. "And now he's gone. He's dead."

"Shut up!" Four eyes turn and look at me, astonished. Even I'm taken aback by my own words. "He's not dead."

"Kalli, I told you not to move. It's not safe."

"I know, that's why we have to find Fallon quickly and get out of here," I say, moving a rock.

"Stop it!" Adalyn screams. "You need to lift them. If you just jostle them, you'll crush him."

"Come on, Addy, we're all trying to help. And this wouldn't have happened if...."

"If what?"

No one speaks. The answer hangs in the air. Ellis and Adalyn move faster, their arms a blur as they pull out rock after rock.

"Shhh." Ellis holds up his hand. "Do you hear that?"

We freeze. I close my eyes, hoping to hear something. Hoping to hear Fallon.

"It's coming from under here," Adalyn says, as she ferociously flings her hands into the pile of rocks and tosses them aside. "Fallon? Can you hear me?"

A low moan winds its way through the spaces between

210

the rocks. Ellis scrambles closer to Adalyn, and together they clear the boulders that have claimed Fallon. His face and chest are covered in blood. Ellis tunnels his hands under Fallon's body, trying to lift him out.

"We need to get out of here before everything gives way," Ellis says.

"There's not enough time," Fallon whispers. "I'll slow you down. Just go."

"No. Fallon, I'm not leaving you. I'm so sorry," Adalyn cries. "I didn't mean what I said. I was just so angry. The baby was yours. Ellis wouldn't." She pauses and looks at Ellis and then at Fallon. "I'm so sorry I hurt you. I never wanted to hurt you. I love you."

"I know you do," Fallon says, his voice barely audible. "It's okay, Addy. But you have to go now."

Adalyn shakes her head, tears falling onto Fallon's face as she leans over him. "I never meant for any of this to happen. I was just so angry and so sad."

"Addy, I know." Fallon coughs and gags.

"I've almost got my hands through this," Ellis says.

"Ellis, stop." Fallon grimaces from the effort of placing his hand on top of his brother's. "It's no good. My legs are crushed."

"No. You don't know that."

"I do. And if you move me anymore, I'll bleed out. It's only the weight of the rock that's keeping me alive."

"It's crushing you. It's not helping you. Listen, we'll get you out and then Margaret can fix you," Adalyn says.

Fallon says nothing. He just shakes his head.

Ellis stops pulling on Fallon. Tears streak his dust-covered cheeks.

"You better get going if there's any chance of making it to those ships. Maybe even saving those women," Fallon gasps.

"I'm not leaving you. This is all my fault," Adalyn says.

And then I remember his pack. I crawl over to Fallon's body and lift up his shirt. He moans from my touch.

"What are you doing? Get off of him!" Adalyn pushes me back.

"His pack—he's got that drink. He gave it you."

"Kalli, that won't work. Not ... for ... this," Fallon sputters. The anguished lines in his face fade, leaving behind a vacant stare. He becomes absolutely still.

"Fallon!" Adalyn's cries are so piercing that I expect the walls and ground to crumble from the weight of her agony.

"It's not safe here. We need to get to the ships and leave," Ellis says.

"Let go of me." She shoves away his hand.

"Addy, he's gone. There's nothing we can do for him."

"Go away."

"He wouldn't want you to die. Come on." Ellis stands up and holds out his hand.

"I'm not leaving him, Ellis. I'm not." Adalyn lies down beside Fallon, her arm resting on his chest.

Ellis says nothing. He takes my hand, and we walk away. Neither of us looks back.

TWENTY-NINE

"Ellis?" I say. "I'm so sorry."

"Please don't. Not now. I can't. Right now all I can do is focus on keeping us alive. We need to get to the spaceships."

Like so many times before, I'm wrapped in Ellis's arms. I'm not sure if it was his fall or the death of Fallon, but his pace is slower and he stops periodically to catch his breath.

"You don't have to carry me. I can run."

He shakes his head. "There's no need to run. The ships should be in that building." He points to a stone structure about two hundred feet away.

We walk quickly, constantly checking to see if we have been discovered. Finally we arrive at the building and rush inside, setting off the alarms.

We stand rooted to the ground as if some invisible tether is holding us fixed to the floor. The siren wails so loudly that my brain shakes and my ears throb. Ellis rushes to a wall, and the blaring stops.

It's a large warehouse holding several spaceships of different sizes. A couple resemble the ship we had been in. Ellis rushes to a bigger ship. It looks like an airplane, with its rounded nose and wings on the sides. He opens a compartment beneath one of the wings.

"We haven't got much time. We need to load the capsule with as many supplies as we can."

There's a line of wide lockers at one end of the building. Ellis yanks open the doors and tosses me package after package, which I fill the compartment with.

"You get on the ship, and I will release the controls," he says.

"Wait. You're not coming?"

"Of course I'm coming. Well, if you want me to."

"I do."

He smiles wistfully. "Here, take these and get on." He hands me a box of syringes.

"What's this for?"

"It's nuveau flureans. I grabbed all I could find. There's not much, but it'll have to do."

The meaning of his words sinks in. I can't let him do this. "You have no way of knowing how your body will react to living on Earth in the long run. Do you? You need this stuff to survive," I say. "There are only a few syringes. We have to stay here."

"It's not safe here. There's too much upheaval. The whole planet could be flooded with molten rock," Ellis says.

"They might be able to stop it. Fallon said Lucas had a team working on it."

Ellis shakes his head. "Many have abandoned Lucas. They're no longer confident he can lead the planet to recovery. We knew this would happen if we failed our mission. And now with the impending volcanoes, I can't take any chances of you getting hurt. Plus we can save those women if we go back."

Then I remember. "The embryos? What about them?"

His body sags, as if the answer is too heavy bear. "I don't know when, or if, they can ever come back to Istriya."

The thought of going back to the basement of the workshop and seeing all of it makes me sick. But I can't let all those women die, just like I can't let Ellis die.

"So send me back alone. You can't survive on Earth without those flureans. I'll figure a way to help those women."

Saying the words tears my heart apart. To live without Ellis? But I don't want him to risk his life for me again. I can't bear the thought of watching him die because he came back to Earth for me.

Ellis pulls me into his arms and lifts my chin. "If going back with you means my life is shortened by ten, fifteen, twenty years, I don't care. If I die tomorrow, I don't care, as long as I get to spend every moment up to my last breath with you."

Ellis grabs my waist and hoists me into the spaceship. Once I'm sitting down, he adjusts my straps, and then he injects me with some more of the flureans. As I watch him fiddle with his straps, I worry about how his body will cope with living on Earth. Maybe it will be okay. It has to be okay.

"Kalli, there's one more thing. Lucas was adamant that no one on Earth be harmed. Even if it meant our identity was discovered. But there are others in the Council who hold different views. And if one of them replaces him, well, it would be best if no one knew we escaped. It would

215

be best if they thought we either perished when the chamber exploded or died trying to escape."

"Ellis?" My voice is small.

In the minimal light I can see his face, ashen and tense. I squeeze his hand, prodding him to speak to me.

"No one can know we left the planet alive. I've set up explosives that are timed to go off so that we can escape unnoticed."

"What are you talking about? This is a huge ship. Of course people will see it." And then the realization sends me reeling. "If they know I escaped, they'll come after me. They'll go to my house. They'll find Navi!"

Ellis flicks switches, and the ship roars to life.

"I won't let that happen," he assures me. "The explosion will be huge. The smoke and flames will completely conceal the ship."

"How? What can you blow up that is so big?"

Ellis rests his arm on one of the levers. "I'm going to blow up the entire building. It's the only way." Ellis's hands frame my face.

"But if there isn't enough smoke to hide us?" I ask.

"Then we don't go."

I nod. He pulls what looks like a tiny silver phone from his pocket. He leans in and kisses me gently on my lips. And then he presses a series of buttons on the phone.

"The explosives are set to detonate in ten seconds. As soon as the first explosion starts, we take off."

I press back into my chair, one hand clenched around the armrest the other wrapped around Ellis's hand. I shut my eyes but immediately open them as the first blast tears up the building, and our ship bursts into the sky.

The world is black. I can't see anything outside of the ship.

"Ellis, how can you fly this thing if you can't see?"

"Hang on, Kalli. We need the smoke to shield our escape. I'm just going straight up."

He pulls his hand from mine and grips the steering wheel.

"Was it enough? Will it hide us?" My voice is urgent.

Before he can answer, the ship is propelled even farther up by another explosion and then another and another. The sound vibrates against my bones. Smoke and flames lash out from all sides. The ship will be transformed into an oven. My fingers dig deep into the arms of the chair.

"It's okay, Kalli. We're still okay," Ellis shouts, over the roar of the flames lapping up the ship. "Almost there. Almost there," he repeats, just as we break through the wall of thick black smoke.

The change is instantaneous, reinforcing the fact that we're traveling at an unbelievable speed. We're surrounded in a beautiful purple haze.

"Ah," Ellis breathes and sits back into his chair. "You okay?"

"I think so. You?"

"I think so."

As the ship takes us back to Earth, I close my eyes. I allow myself to play out my happily ever after. A life where I am safe. A life where there is love. A life where there's

217

still hope for me. And I hold on to that as tightly as I hold on to Ellis's hand.

What lies ahead is full of uncertainties. But at least we're alive. That, in itself, is a miracle. We'll find our way.